Digital Dementia

Max V. Weiss

ISBN: 1500873373
ISBN-13: 978-1500873370

DEDICATION

To everyone who dares to fight the good fight

1.

Monday morning I woke up in a dumpster. It was the old style dumpster. No electric shocks on detection of animal intruders. Or human for that matter. Just a small speaker that screeched a high pitched alarm every hour on the hour. And always just as I was drifting into the good part of a dream. Or lying awake thinking about the past 6 months. Scavenging from hole to hole, crevice to crevice, searching for the perfect getaway, until I ended up here. Still not perfect, but getting closer. The farther I get from society, the closer that perfection gets. Even with the hourly screech, this metal box was preferable to the 7 to 12 world I'd left behind slinging code for Plexol. And while I love nothing more than to piss away endless hours digging into the 1's and 0's, once it became a job, once I was stuck in my tiny cubicle in a warehouse sized room filled with thousands of other cubicles, once I realized I was just another code monkey, the whole experience quickly changed from one of pure joy to pure torture. From 1 to 0. Or 1 to -1.

I lifted the heavy lid and peaked out across a field of mud with the occasional patch of brown grass. About 1 klick south of me there was little more than the foundation of the old Bloom Chocolate factory, sticking up out of the mud. I'd tried the basement as a temporary home, but I would wake up coughing and have fine chocolate powder stuck in my throat all day. Someone really needs to clean that place up so the bums have a nice place to sleep.

I pushed my way out of the dumpster and started walking towards the building to dig out my food stash, but halfway there I spotted another homeless guy curled up about 10 feet from the stash. I whistled to get his attention. Nothing. No movement. It was cold out and the guy didn't even have a coat or a layer of bubble wrap blankets, so he was either drunk or dead. Or both. I came up closer, keeping a nervous eye on him. No movement. Standing over him, I tapped his shoulder with my shoe a few times. He rolled over and opened one eye. I could see his hand reaching into his pocket, and I reached into mine as well, making sure he saw me. He just smiled and pulled out an empty hand. Smart guy. Didn't feel like getting stabbed today. Not that I had anything other than a hand in my pocket. Sometimes a good bluff can save you some headaches. It can save you getting killed, too.

I smiled at him, but kept my hand in my pocket and stepped back a little. Just in case. "This spot is no good. I'm finished with that dumpster up there, you might find it more to your liking."

He eyed me, especially the hand in my pocket, but kept that smile plastered on. "Thanks for the advice, friend. I'm fine right here."

"You'll freeze to death. It's nice and warm in the dumpster. I'm leaving for the day, you can have it as long as you like."

"Thanks all the same, I'm fine."

I fought the urge to glance over in the direction of my food stash. It was singing to me and my empty gut was singing right back.

"You'd be doing me a favor," I said.

"And what if I don't?"

"Nothing. It's just you'd be doing me a favor if you did."

"Well, I'm not in a favor-doing mood today. I like this spot."

My gut was talking louder than I was and I decided I'd just have to dig up my stash and find somewhere new to hide it. I walked away from him and found the stone that marked the place, pushing it away and pulling the wood cover off the hole. My buddy was watching every move, but he wasn't getting up, which was fine by me. Every time I glanced over he'd put that dumb smile back on. But he kept his hand away from his pocket, which was all I cared about. He called over, "looking for something?"

"Never you mind, buddy."

"I can save you some trouble."

"How's that?"

"It's gone. And I ain't the one that grubbed it, so don't get sore. But I saw who did."

I looked down in the hole and it was empty. 5 days' worth of food gone, and me without any credits on my chip. Just perfect. I stared back at his smiling brown teeth.

"Ok, so what did he look like?"

"Well dressed. He ain't one of us. Someone who didn't need whatever you had hid in there."

"Did you talk to him?"

"Hell no. I ain't stupid. I watched. I waited. When he left I looked to see if there was anything else in there. There wasn't, so I closed it back up, figuring I might use the stash myself later. Then I figured, that's no good since it's already been found. And that's when I got cracked."

"Cracked?"

"On the head. Someone come up behind me. Probably the suit. When I came to my head was killing me, and I decided to have a few swigs and sleep it off, which I was doing just fine until you come by."

"How long ago?"

"How the hell should I know? A few hours maybe? It was dark then and now it's light, that's all I know."

I stood staring at him. The fake smile was gone. He pulled his knit cap off to show me his pale bald head and the purple lump with a little crust of blood. He rubbed it gently.

"Still hurts like hell. He didn't need to do that. It's just mean."

"I tend to agree with you, bud."

I reached into my coat and pulled out my flask, uncapped it and handed it over. He took a long pull from it, then handed it back. He reached out his hand and I thought at first he wanted to shake hands but he grabbed hard and pulled himself up on shaky legs.

"Thanks for the drink."

"I appreciate the info, bud, and I always take care of my friends. What's your name?"

"They call me Rube. You?"

"Quint."

"Glad to know you Quint."

"Likewise. Listen, if you happen to see the suit again, I'd appreciate a heads up. I could pay him back for that lump on your head as well as for messing with my stash. I've got an e-drop at quint@xmail.drop."

I wrote it down on a scrap of paper and handed it to him. He tucked it away. I looked at the lump on his head. It looked pretty bad.

"You gonna be ok?"

"A little sleep and I'll be good as gold."

"Well, I'll let you get to it. Like I said, you see anything—"

"I got it. Don't worry, I'm on the cyfi all the time. I got the chip."

He pointed to a small scar just above his left ear. The location was right for a brain chip, but I'd never seen one with a visible scar before.

"That's a pricey bit of gear, where'd you get that done?"

"Prison. Human guinea pig. 5 years ago they were doing the final testing on these. They'd already stuck them in rats and dogs.

In exchange for volunteering they shaved a year off my sentence. Plus I got to keep the chip. Comes in handy. I got the whole cyberverse right here."

He touched the scar with a grubby finger. We stared at each other for a while. Then he coughed.

"Well, guess I'll be getting to it," he said.

"Guess so. Glad to meet you Rube."

"Likewise."

He limped off to my dumpster. I watched him climb in, at one point almost falling off the damned thing. Then, before he lowered the lid he gave me a feeble wave. I turned and walked toward town, figuring I'd stop by my credit chip stash, go buy more food, then find someplace to hide it. Right now the only place I wanted to hide it was in my stomach.

2.

There's bad luck and then there's bad signs. This was turning into the latter. The same guy who raided my food stash had hit my credit stash. There was an apple core sitting where my credit chip had been tucked away, deep inside a hole in the wall in a 3 story abandoned parking garage. Whoever was doing this, they were being blatant and nasty. That left me to wonder who would bother messing with me like this. I'd been drifting for a while without any connection to the straight world, why did they come looking for me now? But why would have to wait. The easier question to answer was who. It had to be someone from Plexol. I'd left enough enemies there to fill a dance hall. The fact that I'd left the dance long ago wouldn't matter to some wise guy who thought I'd slighted him, or been too smart or too successful or too whatever. It was the politics there that finally pushed me out the door. The sea of endless grey cubicles and long hours were bad, but dealing with all those corporate psychopaths could wear you down fast.

And so it was back to the belly of the beast. If they wanted to get my attention they weren't going to give up until they got a reaction. I took the stairs up to the NanoRail station and waited, turning it all over in my mind. There had been 5,000 credits on that chip. There was more in the bank, but the whole point of this 6 months was to see how long I could survive off the grid.

The NanoRail pulled into the station empty. When I passed through the door a voice cracked over the loudspeaker, "you do not have a NanoRail pass, please return to the station to purchase one. I passed my hand through the laser beam in the doorway to make it think I'd gotten off the train. The door closed and off we went.

Plexol had its own station, a gleaming steel, chrome, and glass monstrosity. People movers radiated out towards the various divisions. I headed for Programing 2A, my old home away from home. They had a new girl working the security desk, a petite brunette with bangs, dark eyes peeping out, scanning me up and down. She already had me pegged for a homeless guy and was pushing a button to call one of the meat heads over. I saw him moving towards me on an intercept path between me and the girl, but I was faster and got to the desk. Before I could say anything I could feel his breath on my neck. "Something I can help you with?"

I spoke to the girl, ignoring the meat head. "Hello, I'm Quint Heldin here to see Joth Wilb."

Her lashes flicked at the tips of her bangs. "Is he expecting you sir?"

"I'm not sure. Why don't you ask him that."

The meat head moved closer, laying a fat arm on the desk in

front of me. "No need to be rude to the lady. Why don't we go outside and discuss this?"

"If I wanted to interact with you, it wouldn't be outside. It would be with you behind bars and me tossing you peanuts."

He grabbed my arm and dragged me back to the people mover. I could see Dark Eyes on her communicator. She called out to the meat head, "hey Jimmy, it's ok. Joth is coming down to see Mr. Heldin."

Jimmy let go of me but you could see he wasn't happy about it. He sauntered back to his post, keeping an eye on me while I waited for Joth. I looked around the place expecting to see someone I know walk by, but I didn't recognize a soul. Among the thousands who worked here, I'd only ever really gotten to know a few well. For that matter, there were only a few with recognizable souls. The rest all sort of blended together. And in my present state, it wasn't likely any of them would recognize me.

Joth strolled out of the elevator and half jogged towards me, smiling. "Quint! Good to see you. You look . . . um . . . good to see you."

We shook hands and he led me toward the exit to the parking lot. "Quint, I've been trying to reach you. Let's go take a drive and catch up."

"Trying to reach me? You didn't send a guy out looking for me did you?"

"No. Why, is someone following you?"

"Not sure."

Joth looked around nervously. "That's . . . not good. Let's take a drive."

Joth had obviously done well with Plexol and was driving a new Yugg 1010. Stainless steel exterior, automatic body contouring seats, individualized climate control including oxygen blend, and a top speed of 500 kilometers per hour when driven in aeroglide mode, which keeps the car an inch off the ground on a magnetic cushion. Similar technology to the NanoRail, but without the thin wire needed to guide the train. Instead there were plates embedded in the road to keep the car on course and provide half the magnetic push to keep the car floating. I ran my hand over the smooth black dash. "Nice ride, Joth. Company car or did you spring for this yourself?"

"I'm making payments."

"That surprises me, I always took you for the piggy bank type."

"I am, but I realized to move up in this company you have to look like you've already arrived. This is my 'I've arrived' car."

"How's that working for you?"

"Other than putting 90% of every paycheck into a damned car, pretty good. I'm clawing my way up like everyone else. Plexol seems to enjoy the cat fights and back stabbing. If you ask me it's counterproductive, but then . . . nobody asked me."

"So you said you were looking for me. What's up?"

"First tell me about this tail. Who's following you?"

"Just a hunch. I had a food stash and a credit chip stash. Both raided by some guy in a suit. I didn't see him, but I got a tip. Who knows, maybe the tip was in on it. All I know for sure is someone had to be following me around to know where that stuff was. Someone wanted to mess with me and they did. A message, maybe. I'm not sure."

"Shit."

Joth gripped the steering rod tighter, even though at this point the car was driving itself. He punched a button on the nav panel and the car exited the main road, taking side roads until we were pretty far from downtown. The car pulled up and parked at a diner Joth and I had been to back when he was my boss at Plexol. It was a good place to get away from the office and brainstorm without people listening in and stealing our ideas. We walked in and sat at our old booth, and after the waitress took our order Joth leaned closer, talking in a low voice. "Quint, I need your help. There's some major shit going on and I need someone I trust. Someone outside Plexol. Someone with the hacking skills and inside knowledge you possess."

"What's going on, someone steal your stapler?"

"It's a bit more complicated than that. I assume you're familiar with the brain chip."

"Of course. Instant access to the cyberverse from anywhere. Clever device."

"Well, the best one out there right now is Plexol's and we've been pushing it. The hardware is actually stock, the same device everyone else is using with a few minor upgrades. The secret sauce is in the software."

"I heard you guys are pushing commercials."

"Exactly. To get the price down we supplement the device with advertising, delivered during sleep. The user is aware of the commercial, which is incorporated into a dream seamlessly. Sort of like product placement in the old movies. So that allows us to undersell everyone else, and grab market share like crazy."

"Smart. So who sticks these bugs into people's heads?"

"That's all outsourced. Independent docs. It's actually a very simple procedure, outpatient. Just pop and it's in. The hole heals up in a day. No trace."

"Actually, I just met a fellow today with a little scar over his left ear."

"Must have been a beta unit. The first ones were larger. Anyway, the ones we sell you can't tell that they're there. It's a great product. There's actually bits of your old code in there, come to think of it. Part of the encryption algorithm."

"I'm touched. So what's the problem, you guys making so much money on this chip you don't know where to spend it all?"

"We are, but that's not the problem."

The waitress came by with our food. Omelettes, toast, the works. Joth waited for her to drift back off, then continued talking. "So people have been turning up with memory loss. At first we figured it was just an anomaly, a coincidence. There was no way it could be the device. But then more and more people turned up with the same symptoms. A few had the device removed and the memory loss remained, but didn't worsen. Among those who didn't get the device removed, the memory loss continued to worsen."

"And this was only with Plexol's device?"

"Correct. Not one reported problem with anyone else's."

I shoved my mouth full of eggs and thought it over. "So two possibilities, right? Either corporate sabotage by one of your competitors, or an inside job by some nut. But why? Memory loss. What does that get you. I suppose a public relations nightmare, but there are far easier ways of doing that than hacking into that code. That's a pretty big job. Expensive."

"Well, there's more. We took one of the removed devices and installed it in a test dummy, sort of a functioning brain model. We were able to record messages that were being sent from the device just like the advertising, but this wasn't coming from us. It was more specific instructions, going to a different part of the brain. After the instructions had been learned by that part of the brain, it went into 'erase' mode, blocking out the memory of having been given the instruction."

"So it's this erase mode that mucking up the user's memory?"

"That's our working theory."

More eggs found their way to my gut while I pondered this. "Joth, this is insane. It would take an army of coders just to crack into the OS, let alone write the code they would need to accomplish this. It's beyond anything even Plexol coders would be capable of."

"I'm not so sure. Don't forget, you've been out of the game for a while. The technology just keeps accelerating, day by day. I feel like each morning I wake up in a new world, adjust to the new reality, brace myself for the new challenges and unanticipated consequences. It's all moving faster than our ability to formulate ethics and rules to fit the technology."

Joth stared down at his untouched food, then at my nearly empty plate. "Guess you were hungry. Help yourself to mine, I can't eat. Just talking about this stuff has my stomach spinning."

"Don't mind if I do."

I filled my face and washed it down with hot coffee. It all tasted so good. But what I was hearing was nightmarish. Unbelievable.

"Joth, were you able to decode the messages being fed directly to the brain?"

"Some, not all. It's slow work. The first one we cracked was a simple buy command. A specific brand of freeze dried beets. The next day hundreds of people showed up to buy these damned beets."

"Ok, so if this is an inside job, someone looking to rise through the ranks is beta testing a technology that could control purchase decisions. That would obviously be worth a lot, except that you can't use it. The public outcry, even among these sheep, would be overwhelming. It's crossing the line."

"I tend to agree, although that line is moving all the time."

"The more likely possibility is someone outside Plexol grabbing hold of your installed user base and controlling the users remotely. Located on some island somewhere the law can't touch them. They could sell the rights to purchase decisions to less than reputable manufacturers. All on the down low."

"This is why I need you, Quint. I want you to figure this out before the situation gets worse."

"You mean before the feds get wise to the public health crisis you guys are causing? I doubt you have much time. Even those slugs are going to start taking notice. How many of these chips have you guys installed in people's domes so far?"

"About 500,000."

"Great. 500,000 people headed for Idiotville. I assume you're doing a recall."

"If we have to we will. We've been trying to push a software patch to all the devices that would wipe the rogue code and reinstall the factory default OS. So far, that's been a failure. We send out our patch, and within an hour the virus gets reinstalled over it. Whoever did this, they thought it through."

"Joth, you need to do the recall now."

"Quint, it would take the company down. Our stock price—"

"Have you lost your mind? The stock price hell. These are people's brains you're messing up. Apparently permanently. How rapidly does the memory loss develop?"

"It takes weeks for the first symptoms, from there it develops slowly but steadily. Look, Quint, if a recall were an option, I wouldn't need your help. It isn't. It's not my decision to make, and the decision has already been made. I need you to find out who is behind this. Then we quietly crush them, and go back to business as usual. Not a blip on the radar."

"So what's to keep me from blabbing this to the press myself to force you guys to do a recall?"

"Quint, you know better. Plexol would never stand for that. It would be out of my hands."

"Lovely. So with each passing day that I stumble around looking for an answer, people are losing their minds, just a little at a time."

"You'll be well compensated of course."

"You know I don't give a damn about that. And I don't give a damn about anything Plexol could do to me. You have to put a stop to this."

"Quint, the best I could do, and even this will raise eyebrows, is put a moratorium on new installations."

"You haven't already?"

"No. I told you, we want to keep this quiet."

"You people are the ones that have lost your minds. You know about the problem, know it's getting worse, and haven't taken any step to prevent it. You've got bigger problems than outside hackers."

"I can't change Plexol. I'm doing what I can. No one there even knows I'm getting you involved. They're all sitting on their hands, hoping our coders can solve the problem. But after the patch failed, I'm convinced we need to find the people behind this and stop them."

I got up. "Look Joth, I like you. I always did. But too much corporate culture has blocked up your brain. You talk about ethics, what happened to yours?"

Joth didn't answer. We walked back to his car and got in, driving in silence. Finally Joth turned to me. "So you'll help me?"

"I don't have a choice. That's the only thing that's clear about this situation. But this guy who messed with my stash. Maybe Plexol is a step ahead of you. Or maybe the guy behind this virus. Someone's keeping an eye on me and wants me to know it. Intimidation."

"I can get you protection."

"Who, one of those lobby gorillas?"

"No, I've got someone good. Someone you trust."

I stared at him hard. I knew what was coming, and the feeling in my chest was something I hadn't felt in a long time. Something I didn't want to feel. "Josie? If this is your way of sweetening the deal—"

"Quint, if you have someone else in mind—"

"I haven't had anyone else in my mind for years. But she agreed to this?"

"She will."

"Lovely. You really are a Plexol boy now. The brutal indifference to people's feelings will suit you well as you claw your way to the top. In fact, I'm sure cracking this virus will be a substantial step up the ladder for you."

"Quint, I do care, but I also know what's possible and what isn't. What's reasonable. I'm playing by someone else's rules. It's … tricky."

"Yeah, it's tricky all right. Fine. I can work with Josie. When do we get started?"

"Now. I'm going to drop you off at Maytek Hospital to meet with Dr. Weinberg. He's done hundreds of implantations for us, and he's the one we're using for extractions. Gather whatever useful info you can from him. He's intimately familiar with the brain chip. Then you can get your new place set up and start pouring over code."

"What new place?"

"I got you a room on the outskirts of town. Don't worry, it's a shitty neighborhood, just the type you like."

"You're a funny guy."

He handed me a key chip and a credit chip. "This gets you in the door, and this pays for food and anything else you need. There's 10,000 credits on it, but if you drop below 1,000 it will automatically refill."

"Nice. A little too convenient too. My credit gets stolen, then you show up with a new one."

"Quint, we've known each other a long time. Whatever you may think of me, I'm not that obvious. Someone else messed with your stuff. Let Josie work on that angle. I want you focused on solving the bigger problem."

He gave me a card with my new address written on it and

dropped me off at the hospital. At the info desk they were oddly helpful, directing me to Dr. Weinberg's office. It was a mess, and in the middle of the mess was a wild haired old man with long boney fingers and a thin neck. I introduced myself and we sat down. He pulled a stack of papers from one of many that littered his desk. At least, I assume there was a desk somewhere under there. He looked me over.

"Joth told me you'd be coming."

"Well, that explains the friendly reception."

"I have a lot to tell you, but I'm expected in surgery in a little while. You can take this and read it on your own time."

He handed me the stack of paper. I flipped through it quickly. "You don't have this scanned?"

"Some things are better left analog, Mr. Heldin."

"Please, call me Quint."

"Here's what you need to know. I've started working with a group of post-extraction patients. As I'm sure Joth told you, the memory loss they suffered after implantation of the Plexol BC1965 remains stable. I did brain scans to look for tissue damage or other observable changes to the affected area. Nothing. I ran several other diagnostic tests looking for other deficits, including sensory, balance, eye hand coordination, etc. Nothing."

"So what's that tell you?"

"Nothing."

"Ok, so now what?"

"I'm working on reversing the damage, but that's pretty

difficult to do when I can't find any objective evidence of the damage beyond the consistent self-reporting of the patients of chronic loss of short term memory input."

"So it doesn't affect long term memory?"

"Not as far as I can tell. A typical manifestation would be you set down your keys, then completely forget where you put them. Or forget where you parked your car, or why you went to the store. Of course, these things happen to everyone, but in the post implantation group the occurrence is anywhere from 100 to 1,000 times more prevalent, and where they fall in that spectrum coincides with the how long they've had the brain chip implanted."

"So you know it's the chip, and you know what it's doing."

"But I don't know how to prevent it or treat it. My two top priorities right now are discrete extraction and reversal of damage. The first is easy. I've probably done about 20-30% of the implantations. I'm merely scheduling my former patients for a follow up visit, at which time I test their memory, and tell them we need to extract the device due to a defect. At no charge of course. After extraction I schedule them for more follow up visits during which time I attempt to reverse the damage."

"How?"

"Various methods, most involving a brain stimulator that has been successful in reversing various age, disease, and injury related memory loss."

"What's your success rate?"

He frowned and stared off into space. "Zero. It's a nontrivial challenge given the lack of identifiable objective evidence of brain damage. I'm basically shooting blind."

"Well doc, all this is interesting, but I don't see how it helps me with what I need to do."

"You're assuming I know what that is. Joth was fairly oblique."

"Probably a good idea. The less you know the better. Let's just say you and I are working on the same team."

"Of course. That's why I've given you those papers. I hope you'll find something in there helpful. And of course, I am at your disposal if you have any specific questions."

"I appreciate it."

We shook hands and he showed me to a corridor that led to a skyway, then to the NanoRail. I loaded up a ride chip figuring I'd be needing it, and rode out to take a look at my new digs.

3.

The building looked run down on the outside, but inside the apartment was a large loft space with plenty of room to spread out. Windows looked out toward the entrance, and on the other side was an exit to a fire escape. Joth had obviously thought this through. It would be a good place to hide out, and easy to see if I was being watched. The building had cyfi, but I prefer a wired connection if I'm going to dive into the cyberverse, and so I was happy to see a jack in the wall. Now all I needed was something to plug into it. I needed something powerful enough to crack a few encryption algorithms, but old enough to not have a government mandated GPS chip. I had an idea where to find the right gear, but first I sat down with Dr. Weinberg's stack of paper, spreading it out on the floor and looking it over for anything helpful. There were some technical specs for the brain chip, but nothing regarding Plexol's software. I decided to leave the heavy reading for later and jumped back on the NanoRail.

10 stops later I was at the MicroMax Mall. It was the type of

place I generally avoid, an instant hangover of flashing lights, animated interactive displays calling out to you at every step, doors whooshing open and closed as you walk by, highly caffeinated sales people at your elbow every 5 seconds asking if they can help you. I found the place dizzying.

The place was packed with the usual brainwashed sheep, popping in and out of shops with armsful of useless freshly purchased crap. They walk in a daze of auto-erotic consumerism that keeps them in the seemingly endless downward spiral of work, earn, spend, work, earn, spend. At the bottom of the spiral their mortal coil gets flushed down the electronic toilet while the heaps of shiny plastic nothing gets left behind. It was the last place on earth I wanted to be, but the man I needed to see had a little shop there, tucked in a quarter sized space squeezed between a day spa and a luggage store.

When I walked in Frank didn't seem to recognize me. It had been years, and my attire was a little different from what I wore in my coding days. But as I approached the counter his eyes registered surprised recognition. "Quint?"

"How's it been, Frank."

"Still alive, I guess. You look half alive so I guess I'm doing better than you."

"I've been off the grid a while. Surviving."

"Something to do I guess. If you're looking for a laser shaver, I don't sell them."

I rubbed my bristley jaw. "It's on the to do list, but not

today. I need an older laptop. Powerful, but no US-GPS chip."

"Quint, you know I can't carry anything like that."

"I thought there was some loophole about building your own."

"I can build it, just can't sell it."

"How's about I steal it."

"I think there might be a law against that too."

"How about I make a donation to your favorite charity, and you give me a nice gift."

"That could work. But I'm taking a chance."

"I'll make it worth your while."

He looked me up and down, saw that I was serious, and disappeared into a back room. A few minutes later he came out with a pizza box, which judging from the way he carried it had something a little heavier than a pizza in it. "I can't finish this, you take it."

"Can do. What do I owe you?"

"Let's call it 4,000 credits."

"Done."

"Done? I thought you would haggle a little. You back on the corporate teat?"

"Sure, that's why I dress so nice."

I paid him and left with the "pizza", trying to blend in with the crowd and failing miserably. By the time I got home it was raining out and I was running with the pizza box stuck under my jacket. When I walked into the apartment she was sitting on the floor, waiting for me.

"How long you been waiting for me, Josie?"

"I just got here myself. I've been trailing you since you got to the hospital."

"I guess I'm losing my touch. So how'd you get in."

"It's pretty high tech stuff, Quint. You forgot to lock the door."

"Nice. I really am losing my touch. So . . . I've missed you."

I was sorry I said it but it was true and now it was out there. She stood up and walked over to me, placing a warm hand on my cheek. "You need a shave Quint. And a shower."

"So tell me something I don't know."

"Ok." The hand pulled away, leaving a cold longing in its place. "You told Joth about some guy who messed with your stash."

"Stashes. Joth never listens."

"Same could be said about you, baby. Anyway, I saw a guy in a suit following you after you left the hospital. I took the opportunity to introduce myself, but he didn't seem very friendly. Tried to jump me, but we all know how that usually ends."

"One of a few ways if I recall correctly, but I'm guessing in his case it didn't end on his desk with office supplies thrown to the floor."

"You're cute, Quint. I let him lay down where he stood and take a rest by himself. Searched him. Ever see this?"

She pulled a card from her pocket. Embedded in the center was a chip with a strange symbol on it, sort of a crescent with a wave through it. I turned it over in my hand.

"Never have. It's not Plexol. And they've got enough guys working dirty for them they wouldn't need to reach out to an independent. What's the chip?"

"I was hoping you'd figure that out. You're the hacker."

"We both are Josie."

"You were always more into it than I was. Hunched over your computer 24 hours a day."

"Goddamn I think I've heard this before."

"Sorry Quint, I didn't mean it that way."

I took a long look at her. Those same sad eyes that could break my heart every second of the day. Long straight black hair, and a body more poised for action than any panther stalking prey. She handed me the card and I took it along with my pizza box to the kitchen counter. Inside the box was a heavy laptop. I knew the shell but I was sure Frank had gutted and restored the innards. He always kept a few of these souped up specials around. I never knew what he used them for, and I never asked.

The machine booted fast, presenting me with a customized OS. I'd seen it before. Another flavor of Frank's tweaked system. I was in familiar territory, although I had a feeling he'd done further tweaking since the last time I'd delved into one of his computers. Josie drifted closer and watched over my shoulder as I slid the chip card into the reader and loaded up some diagnostic programs. They attacked it from several angles and each offered up its results. So far, nothing too stellar. Chip manufacturer, running an unknown code base, last modified today. Josie pointed to a line of code on the screen. "Looks like a key chip."

"Could be. Could be lots of things. I've seen that same process in a million different applications. What's more interesting is the short term storage. I think our friend files his report to whoever pulls the strings with this card. He must carry a device to input the information. He didn't have anything else on him?"

"Nothing."

"Ok, then he's going somewhere, a home base, a remote location, maybe one of several where this gives him access to a device, or a room where the device is located. He uses that to input his report, and to send it. Probably wipes the message as soon as its sent."

"So there won't be any useful data on there."

"I didn't say that. There's wiping data and then there's wiping data. This type of chip continues to have a residue of the data even after several wipes with random strings of 1's and 0's. Depending on how thorough this guy is, I might be able to revive his most recent report, even get a clue of where it was sent. Of course, I'll have to crack the encryption on the message. Again, that will depend on how thorough he's being. But so far this is the best shot we have to finding out who is behind all this."

"You're assuming that whoever put a tail on you is also involved in the brain chip virus."

"That I am. It's the most logical conclusion at this point. If you've got a better theory, don't be shy."

Josie walked toward the door. I couldn't help watching. The entire room seemed to sway a little with each step. She turned and locked eyes. She'd used this look on me a million times, and it always worked.

"If you need me, I'm across the hall. Just knock, yell, scream. Whatever the situation calls for."

"Thanks. What happens if I whistle."

"You probably get smacked in the face."

"I might take you up on that sometime."

"Oh, and I almost forgot. I have a present for you."

She reached into her coat pocket and pulled out a gun. Not a normal laser gun. This thing was a relic. Shiny silver, totally mechanical. I'd fired a few like this when I was a kid. They're loud and kick back when you shoot them. A little lead bullet spits out and tears a little chunk out of whatever or whoever you point the thing at. Fun stuff. Josie handed it to me. "It's in mint condition, and I just cleaned and oiled it for you. Sig Sauer P232. Compact, but deadly if you hit the vitals. Even if you miss, it makes a big enough bang to scare the shit out of whoever happens to be bothering you."

"Thanks kid. Now I feel bad I didn't get you anything."

"Just stay alive, Quint. That can be your present to me."

"I'll make a point of doing that."

I took a closer look at the gun. It was a precision machine. The type of thing no one bothered to make or appreciate anymore. It was perfect. I watched the room sway again as Josie made her exit. When she was gone I got back to work on cracking the card chip. I took a break and sifted through Dr. Weinberg's papers, then stashed them away in the kitchen cabinet. I went back to working on the chip card, but was still getting nowhere. After a few fruitless hours I decided to grab some air and a gulp of coffee.

It was pitch black out and quiet. In the distance you could see the lights of the city and hear the hum of traffic. I walked toward that hum, figuring there had to be a coffee shop somewhere between here and there. I kept an eye over my shoulder just in case. The feel of the hard steel gun in my pocket was reassuring. In my head the lines of code were still flashing by. I hadn't even managed to salvage anything from the erased portion of the chip, let alone start working on the encryption. Maybe this wasn't the best approach. Maybe finding the guy who was tailing me before was the best bet. Maybe, subconsciously, I already knew that. Maybe that's why I was out walking around a crappy neighborhood in the middle of the night. Or maybe it was to try and shake the scent of Josie out of my nostrils. That girl had a way of working herself into my system. She was my virus. Maybe that sounds harsh, but there's no denying she'd done me more harm than good. And she's done me a hell of a lot of good. It's just, somehow, I always end up regretting it.

Up the street was a small diner, the type with bad coffee and greasy food. My kind of place. Through the glass I could see her sitting at a booth, looking right at me and sipping her water. Across the table the waitress was setting down a hot cup of coffee, steam curling off and drifting away. I walked in and sat down, took a swig, and stared at those damned sad eyes. "You know, it drives me nuts when you do that."

"What?"

"Show up wherever I'm going before I get there."

"You walk too slow. And you're pretty damned predictable, Quint. Talk about creatures of habit. You're more a creature of ruts."

"Thanks Josie, that's real sweet."

"Let's get something straight, Quint, I'm not here to be sweet, I'm here to keep you out of trouble while you figure this thing out."

"That's fine by me."

"Is it?"

"Don't start."

She looked down at her hands, then out the window. Those dark eyes, scanning scanning scanning. "Sorry Quint."

"Forget it. Look, I've been thinking. Maybe we let the shadow catch up with me and squeeze him for some info."

"I already thought about that. If these guys have him communicating with a chip card, he probably doesn't even know who the hell he's working for. Probably picked up the card at a drop and gets his credits through it. I'd be surprised if he even knew his own name, let alone who's paying the bills."

"Yeah, you're probably right. Still . . ."

"If the opportunity presents itself . . ."

"Right."

"I take it you haven't made much progress with the chip card"

"Nothing."

"So take another angle. What about the symbol on it?"

"I forgot about that."

"I didn't. While you were sifting through code I did a little research. There are no stock cards out there with that symbol, so someone is either manufacturing their own chip cards or going to the bother of printing that symbol on blanks they get from a normal supplier."

"Why would someone do that. It only improves our chances of connecting them with the card."

"So what's that tell you, Quint."

"The guy that's running this show is an egomaniac. So bent on leaving his mark that he's willing to pay a little risk into the game. You know, you're on the right track here. We actually have a lot of usable info to profile this guy. He obviously knows code, knows chip tech, and he knows enough about Plexol to hack into their system and keep them from reversing the hack. There aren't many people capable of that."

"So now what?"

"I get a list from Joth of disgruntled high end coders that left Plexol in the 2 or 3 years before this happened. Start working my way down the list till we find a ringer."

"Sounds like a brilliant plan."

"You already had this worked out, didn't you?"

She looked out the window again. "It's teamwork, Quint."

"Like hell. You always did like using Socratic method on me."

"Whatever works."

I finished my coffee and got up. She stayed where she was. I asked her, "You coming with?"

"I'll be there before you."

"I don't like that. Walk with me."

"I thought we were trying to catch a shadow. That's not gonna happen with me tagging along."

"Always 10 steps ahead of me. I'll see you there."

4.

Somehow, the dark seemed darker and the coolness in the air just a little cooler. I tried to figure out where Josie was, but soon gave up. She was a born tracker, an invisible ninja, and a heart breaker all rolled into one sweetly seductive package. I decided to shift my attention to finding my shadow. Maybe Josie had conked him a little too hard on the head and he'd drifted off to join the angels. Or maybe without his card, he wasn't getting paid, so why bother. Then again, if I were him, I'd be trying pretty hard to get that card back.

And that's when it struck me. I was now secondary to the all-important card, which I'd left unguarded at the loft. I started running and kept on running until I got there. I ran around back and took the fire escape up, trying to be both fast and quiet. The key chip unlocked the door, and I pulled it open slowly, looking around. The lights were on. Had I left them on? I couldn't remember. I put my hand on my gun and started to pull it out when I saw Josie. She was holding an empty pizza box. "I hope you can use this because it's all you have left."

"Tell me you're kidding."

"I wish I were."

"Just tell me anyway, just so I can feel good for a second. Do it for me."

"No can do. I never was a good liar."

"Sometimes I wish you were."

"Me too."

We both sat down on the floor and sat in our shared cloud of dejection. This was not a good start. I turned to Josie. "Ok, then at least tell me I remembered to lock the door this time."

"Actually, no, you didn't. But I did. I checked both doors before I tracked you to the diner."

"Any sign of a break in?"

"Nope, he hacked the lock somehow."

"Well, the good news is there's nothing on that laptop that will help him. The bad news is, he's got his chip card back and I've got nothing. Should we go look for him?"

"Pointless, he had to be waiting for us to leave. We were gone long enough for him to hack in, get the gear, and blow before you even had your first sip of coffee."

I felt in my pocket. I still had the credit chip Joth had given me. At least there was that. Still, I felt like an idiot. It didn't help that Josie was there to watch me feel like an idiot. Then I remembered the papers. I ran to the kitchen and looked in the cabinet. Dr. Weinberg's stack of paper was still there. "Well, at least he missed this."

"Silver lining. Do me a favor, promise me you'll stay put the rest of the night. I could use some shut eye."

"Sure thing, kid. I could probably use some myself. Tomorrow's another day, right?"

"Tomorrow's today. It's 4 in the morning, Quint."

"Fair enough. Sweet dreams, Josie."

"You too."

I watched her go, and long after she was gone I stared at the place she'd been. I thought through everything that had happened with us, then everything that had happened today. Was I slipping up because of her, or was I just out of practice, living in dumpsters for too long. Either way, I needed to get focused.

There was a mattress against a wall, still wrapped in plastic. I tore open the plastic, gave the mattress a kick, and laid down. At first my mind was still working through the various bits and pieces, but then it all smeared together and I dropped off to sleep. I was slow to wake up until I noticed the laser gun pressed against my head.

5.

There was a man in a suit looking down at me. He seemed nice enough. As long as he didn't pull the trigger. He backed up a little and sat down, keeping the laser gun pointed at me. "Mr. Heldin."

"Quint. And you are . . . "

"They call me Kett."

"Who's they?"

"Well, that's part of what I'm here to talk about. Making us all part of one big us."

"Sounds cozy."

"Could be."

"I'm guessing the pitch involves the idea that I'm not being given a choice in the matter."

"Don't be so grim. My guess is once I've explained it you'll see things our way. No coercion needed. Just logic."

"I'm a big fan of logic. Not much of a fan of that blaster."

He lowered the gun but kept it handy. He tried a smile, then gave up on that. "Let's get to business. The people I work for are the future. Plexol is the past. We were going to invite you to join us and then Plexol got to you first. So now you've been infected by their view of the situation. But their view is clouded and antiquated."

"Let me guess. Your view is all sunny skies and clean diapers."

"I'll leave that up to you to decide after you hear me out."

"One question first. Do you even know who you're working for?"

"I know their work. Not their identities. But what difference does that make?"

"Just you're the spokesperson, trying to sell me on a product you've never seen."

"Oh, I've seen the product. It's just the people behind it that remain . . . anonymous."

"And you think those two things can just be separated out like that? Any product bears the imprint of the maker. The person behind it shapes it in a way that makes the difference as wide as the one between good and evil."

"I'm not interested in getting into philosophy with you Mr. Heldin."

"Quint."

"I'm here to talk business."

"It's all connected, Kett. The people who don't get that are the dangerous ones. All this technology, it's meaningless by itself. Just a puppet. It's the puppeteer that matters. The laser in your gun could be used to cut parts for a life support machine, or to shoot the person who will need that machine to live. It all depends on the man behind the curtain."

He gave me a queer look and I laughed. "You'll have to forgive me if my reference is a little cloudy and antiquated."

"Quint, you and I have more in common than you realize. More importantly, you have more in common with the man who's running this new company than you realize. He wants you on board. It could work out very well for you."

"You know what would work out well for me? If hundreds of thousands of people weren't losing their memory."

"That's just a glitch. We're working on it. It would be easier if Plexol would stop tampering with our code and just let us fix the problem ourselves."

"You got a timeline for that fix?"

"It's one among many priorities. It's being worked on."

"Right. Kind of like I figured. Well, it's my only priority at this point, so unless your boss is willing to bump it up to the top of his to do list, we don't have much to talk about."

"I'm beginning to see why you were kicked out of Plexol, Mr. Heldin. You're only willing to play if you get to call the shots."

"You got some bad information, buddy. I left Plexol by choice, no one pushed me out."

"Forgive me. You know how these rumors spread."

"Yeah, some jackass like you starts making shit up. Are we done here?"

"No. Since you're not willing to listen to reason, I need to go to plan B."

"Coercion?"

"Elimination. We can't allow you to tamper with our work. Plexol can bumble along all it wants, they'll never figure out what's going on until it's too late. You, on the other hand, have the potential to do some mischief. I'm afraid I can't allow that."

He lifted the laser gun and pointed it right between my eyes. "I'd like to say I enjoyed our little talk. But I didn't."

I saw a flash, but not the flash of a laser. It was sunlight reflecting off a knife that flew through the air and landed with a jolt in Kett's right hand. He dropped the gun, but before it even hit the floor Josie had run from across the room and wrestled Kett to the ground. She had him pinned before I could even stand up. I picked up the laser and stuck it in my pocket, then smiled at Josie.

"Good morning."

"It's not going so bad."

"How much of that did you hear?"

"All of it. I thought the conversation was getting a little stale, so I figured I better spice it up."

"Glad you did. I think I was about to die from the boredom."

"Seemed that way."

"So Kett, I've got a lot of questions for you."

He groaned. Josie had him in some sort of pressure point hold. I pulled out the Sig Sauer and leveled it at him. "Let him up so we can have a more interesting chat."

She backed away. Kett sat up and stared down the barrel of my gun. "What the hell is that?"

"You don't want to find out," I said. "First question, what's causing the memory loss?"

"I don't know."

"How close are they to fixing the problem?"

"I don't know."

"What's their ultimate objective?"

"I don't know."

"Ok, that's all the questions I had. I think now it's Josie's turn. Unfortunately for you."

Josie wasted no time. She was all fists, elbows and knees. Kett put his hands up but never managed to block a single blow. She was too fast, too unpredictable. He balled up on the floor but she kept at him. I had a hard time watching it. "Hey Josie, take a break. Let's search the guy, get the card back."

She pulled his jacket off and tossed it to me. She searched him while I went through the jacket and found the card. She pulled a programmable key chip out of his pocket and tossed it to me. That must have been what he used to get into my place. Nice piece of gear, but it doesn't require much know how to use. This guy wasn't a hacker, just a low level action man. I already knew we weren't going to get anything useful from him, so I took the chip card and stuck it into my pocket. "I'm going to get another laptop and start working on this thing again. If you want to stay here and pulp him a while longer, be my guest."

"That's not my job, Quint. Just having fun. If you leave I need to go too. So what do we do with well-dressed Kett?"

"Maybe he can lead us back to my laptop, save me the bother of getting a new one."

Kett peered cautiously up at us. "Let me go and I can give you the laptop."

Josie and I looked at each other. I already knew what she was thinking, and she knew that I knew. That was the thing about her. She could read me like an e-screen. That had gotten me into trouble with her plenty of times. That and the fact I could never really lie to her. Not well enough, anyway.

Kett led us to his stash. Aside from the laptop there were a few more weapons, and the communicator he used to contact his higher ups. I grabbed these while Josie took Kett behind a building. I heard a crack. Then the lid of a dumpster squeaked open. There was a thunk, then the lid squeaked closed again. Josie came back. She saw the look on my face and her eyes narrowed. "It had to be done Quint."

"Knowing that doesn't make it any easier for me."

"I'm not here to make things easy for you, I'm here to protect you."

"So, where to now?"

"Obviously they'll send someone else looking for you. The apartment is out of the question. We need somewhere they'll have a harder time finding us."

"How about the belly of the beast?"

She thought this over. I could see her playing out every

contingency, then backtracking and travelling down another one. I loved her mind, loved everything attached to it. She was a perfect package.

Suddenly I was aware of her watching me watch her. "Ok Quint, but we can't let anyone know, not even Joth. We need to find a way in, then burrow into some long forgotten corner where you can get your work done."

"We've got the shadow's pROM key chip. That can open a few doors for us. The trickier part is getting them to stay shut once we're in. It's safe to assume this group has people embedded at Plexol, all they have to do is set them in motion and our little nest is a trap."

"Well, at this point I don't have a better option. Let's get inside Plexol and see if we can find a usable space. You have a way to approach the building without a million security cameras seeing us?"

It was my turn to crank up my thinker. "The best screen we've got is the crowds coming in from the NanoRail. We blend in, get inside, and . . ."

"Yeah?"

"I'm still thinking. They've got freaking security cameras everywhere. Actually, that could help us if we had access to the monitors. There have to be blind spots. If we tapped in to the monitors we would know when we were out of range. That might expose a vulnerability that gets us in undetected."

"Ok. You can do that?"

"Let's assume the cameras aren't hard wired. There has to be a signal being broadcast. Encrypted of course, but probably not very well, since there's nothing much to hide and it's a steady stream that needs to be decrypted in real time. We get close enough for me to find a crack in the encryption, we pull up the images, go from there."

"That's good Quint, but what if the cameras *are* hard wired."

"Then we come up with a new plan."

She sighed, but it was the best we had. On the way to Plexol she made me stop at a department store where I got some new clothes. Josie wanted to throw my old ones out, but I wouldn't let her. We got back on the NanoRail and took it to the station one stop before Plexol. We found a small park. Trees, fountain, birds. Nice and quiet. She sat next to me on a bench while I hunched over the laptop. I ran some radio scanning routines until I found several continuous encrypted streams. I chose one to work on the encryption and had it cracked in less than half an hour. From there it was just a few minutes before I had all the camera streams cracked and feeding to my monitor, where I could see them all at once or switch between them. In all there were probably a thousand external cameras. There had to be even more internal ones, but I wasn't getting a signal from them, which meant they were hard wired. So getting inside the building was doable, but from there we would be sitting ducks. Josie looked at my screen, then looked at me. "Well?"

"There's a problem."

"I see that. So what do we do once we're inside?"

"I know what the cameras look like. The inside ones are pretty dated. They were installed back when the building went up about 20 years ago. You can see them. Little black domes on the ceiling, about the size of your thumb. They never bothered to hide them, they were happy reminding us that we were being watched all the time. Part of the corporate culture, I guess."

"Ok, so we can see the camera, how do we avoid it?"

"We don't. They've got too many inside cameras to have actual people watching them. It's done by computer, which runs a simple AI routine looking for anything unusual. If it finds something, that gets kicked to an actual human to review."

"What qualifies as unusual?"

"A fight, a fire, explosion. I actually worked on a small piece of the code when I first started there, upgrading it. I think I took it from crappy to less crappy. The real security is on the outside. Once we're in we just act normal so we don't trip off the software."

"And you think that will work?"

"Worst case scenario, we end up in jail for trespassing."

"I don't like that scenario."

"In that case, don't fight, light a fire, or create an explosion once we get in there."

"All right wise guy, let's just do it."

"That's the spirit."

I detached the screen from the laptop and kept it where I could see it inside my coat as we approached the building. Josie walked in front of me to cover the odd bulge in my coat, and I would direct her left or right as we moved through the crowd. There was a fire exit at ground level behind some bushes and I started heading that direction, but the closer we got the more cameras we were showing up on. There were no dead spots. We changed course and headed back into the crowd coming off the NanoRail. Then Jose turned around and whispered to me, "how about that vent?"

I saw where she was looking. About 20 feet out from the building, some sort of exhaust vent in the ground. A few people walked by or over it every few seconds.

"Ok, we can check it out, but even if the camera's aren't on it, people will notice us lifting the grate and climbing down."

"I might have a way. Let's check it out."

We walked a circuitous path to the vent, changing direction every time we came into camera view. Finally, we were standing right on top of the grate. I checked and re-checked every camera. Nothing. It was a dead spot. I leaned closer to Josie. "Ok, we're invisible to the cameras. Now make us invisible to all these people."

"Easy."

She reached into her pocket and pulled out one of the weapons we'd grabbed from Kett's stash. It was a laser grenade on a small handheld launcher. I'd never used one, but she obviously had. There were five buttons on the handle and a small readout. She punched in some numbers, then held the three middle buttons down, pointed the grenade toward a small manmade lake about 50 feet away, then pushed a fourth button. There was a muted "thunk" sound, then a whisper, followed by a bright loud explosion as the grenade touched the water. The explosion vaporized enough water to create a nice big steam cloud and the sound was deafening. I was standing dazed gawking at the explosion when I felt Josie grab me and jump. Before I knew it, we were down in the vent system and she had the grate back in place above us. I felt a little shaky, but ran along behind her as she made her way through the vents. They were obviously built big enough for maintenance people to get into and out of easily and there were even outlets for them to plug gear into. I caught up to Josie and grabbed her arm to slow her down, then whispered to her, "hey, why not right here?"

"Here?"

"Yeah, forget finding a room in the building, this is perfect."

"What if maintenance comes along."

"They would only come down here if the computer signals a problem. We just find the piece of code that handles the fault detection in this vent, tweak it, and we're safe as a sow in a gutter."

"Quint, where on earth do you come up with this stuff?"

"I don't know. I think I read too much when I was a kid. Anyway, let's get to work."

"You get to work, I'll figure out where we can sleep without crippling ourselves."

Josie went searching down the vent and followed a few branches. I suspected that she was more interested in finding an escape if we needed one than a place to sleep. Always the practical one.

I set up my laptop and slid the chip card back in, trying to dredge up any wiped information that I could sort through. Once the program was running there wasn't much for me to do so I covered up the laptop with an old rag I found and went looking for Josie.

The vents branched out in several directions, and following any branch led to more branches. Smaller vents ran up between walls, and where they opened into an office space you could see a little light filtering in. Despite this it was getting pretty dark the further I walked. I doubled back and returned to the laptop to check my progress. Nothing yet. I walked back toward the grate where we'd entered. I could hear sirens. Obviously Josie's explosion had drawn a bit of attention. I just hoped none of the security cameras had picked up the direction from which the laser grenade was launched, as that would lead straight to our current location.

Josie came back carrying a bag. "Hungry?" She opened it up and pulled out containers of food.

"Nice work, where on earth did you get this?"

"I found one of the kitchens. There was nobody in there, so I helped myself."

"You have to be careful of cameras, Josie. Someone popping out of a vent and stealing food is going to draw a little attention."

"Give me a little credit, Quint. The room was pitch black and there were big steal counters I kept between me and the camera. I know what I'm doing."

"I know you do. It just seems like you're getting a little reckless lately."

"What, the grenade? Listen, the longer we were zig zagging around out there, the more likely we were to be spotted. We needed a diversion and I supplied it. If you had a better plan you should have spoken up."

"I'm just saying, we can't be on the run all the time. We need to find a place that's relatively safe and then stay under the radar."

"You let me worry about that. You worry about that chip."

"That . . . chip. Dammit!"

"What's wrong."

"I'm wasting all this time staring at a laptop when I could be looking through the papers Dr. Weinberg gave me. And like an idiot I left them back at the apartment."

Josie pulled out a thick roll of paper from inside her coat. "I grabbed them, Quint."

"Josie, I take everything I said back."

She handed me the papers, which I spread out on the floor. I picked up some pages that explained the internal transmitter. Apparently, while this was primarily an input device, it could also transmit information. As I read more I realized the purpose of this was to request information and confirm receipt of that information. But I wondered, what else could it transmit. A person's thoughts? What they were looking at, hearing, sensing? I grabbed some food out of the bag and filled my gut while studying over the information before me. Josie disappeared back down a long hallway, into the blackness.

Hours passed. Occasionally I'd glance over at the laptop, but there was no progress. What I was learning from the Weinberg papers was interesting, but in the back of my head I realized I was no closer to finding the person behind all this. I remembered talking to Josie about putting together a list of people who matched the profile we'd put together. And as this thought arose, almost on cue, Josie reappeared from the tunnel. "Hey Quint, catch."

She tossed me a chip card. It was a standard Plexol storage card. I plugged it into a free spot on the laptop and opened the only file on it. A list. I looked up at Josie, "How on earth did you pull this off?"

"Easy. I found my way up to Joth's office. You should have seen the look on his face when I whispered his name from the vent in the wall. I told him what we needed, he put it together, loaded it onto that chip, 'accidentally' kicked the chip over to the vent where it fell into my hot little hand."

"And everyone on here matches our profile?"

"Of course."

"Nice work, kid."

"That's what I'm known for."

I looked over the list on my screen. A few were people I'd worked with before, most were unknown. They'd risen through the ranks after I'd jumped off the treadmill. There was enough biographical info on each person to get started narrowing down the list. Some didn't have the coding experience they would need, some were too high up in the Plexol hierarchy to risk it all on a scheme like this. I got the list down to 10 people and ranked them in order of most to least likely. At the top of the list was Sal Templin, a guy I'd worked with before. He had a bad temper. Impatient guy when it came to people, but he could sit and code for hours without moving. I'd seen his work and considered him one of the top coders there. According to the list he'd been bumped up to project manager, which was the type of huge mistake Plexol was good at. Take a guy who's great at code but a total misanthrope, move him to a position where he's doing relatively no coding but managing people. Brilliant.

The list had addresses. I pulled up a map on the laptop and plotted out a course that would place my top suspects near the beginning, but take into account proximity. Fortunately, most code monkeys liked to settle in the hip part of downtown, so there wasn't much distance between them. Josie was looking over my shoulder. "Looks like we're going trick or treating tonight."

"I am. These people will talk to me alone, but not with you along. They don't know you. They'll at least have heard of me."

"Don't worry, I wasn't going to spoil your little shop talk sessions. But I'll be around just in case."

"Works for me. Just lay off the laser grenades for a while."

"Hey, who got you that list?"

"I know, I know. I'm just kidding around, Josie. I, um,

appreciate your help."

"Wow, flatter me why don't you."

She sat down in front of the laptop. "You got something."

I looked. It wasn't much, but slowly the program was mining deeper into the card and pulling up some previously erased data. After a while it looked like one solid chunk of code. I copied it over to the decryption software and let it rip. As the software ran it would start down various blind alleys, and I would re-route it toward what looked like more promising possibilities. In theory, it could take years to crack any decent encryption, but if you've done it a few million times you start to see the patterns, start to recognize what you're looking at. My mind locked in on the task. It was like shooting the rapids, a stream of wild data spewing froth and waves, but heading to one logical destination. All I had to do was avoid the rocks, stay on course.

Little by little I was turning this digital mush into an intelligible message. Then, all at —once, it kicked over and there was the plain text staring me in the face. It was Kett's most recent report to his puppet master. The header indicated where he had sent it from, but what I was more interested in was where it ended up. The destination was represented by a string of letters and numbers. These were randomly assigned for any communication, but each was held in a database. Each was unique. Granted, it more likely pointed to a mobile device than a physical location, but it was better than nothing.

I grabbed the destination code and plugged it into a

program that could surreptitiously access the database. The risk here was leaving digital fingerprints that someone could trace back to me. But it was a risk I had to take. After a few seconds it came back as a car code, which only told me it was a mobile device in a car. No make or model. No year. Just a car. So far, not so useful. I cross referenced with a database of all in-car communications that occurred at that time within a 10 mile radius. There were over 100,000. But most of these were just signals that cars send out for navigational purposes. This made them very short. My message, by comparison was longer. It would have taken a few extra milliseconds to transmit and receive. So I ranked the list of communications by duration, took the top 100, and plotted those on a map. I then superimposed this map on the map of suspects. Not surprisingly, both were clustered downtown. Nothing really jumped out at me.

I pulled the text of the report. It was just a fragment. "Q located at building, will engage and—". Not much help there. Josie watched over my shoulder while I worked, but said nothing. I looked up at her. "Well?"

"I'm seeing the same thing you are. A whole lot of nothing."

"This was a waste of time. We need to get working on this list."

"I thought that had to wait until tonight."

"Josie these people all work late. Some of them never go home. And they're all sitting right on top of us, right now. I need another approach to this."

"Ok, what's that."

I thought a moment. "Go back to Joth. Get me a security pass. I'll walk in the front door and go talk to these people directly."

"Sounds risky."

"It's not like I'm going to walk up and ask if they're the culprit. I just need to get a sense of where their head is at. Maybe hint that I suspect them. Talk about the brain chip and watch their reaction."

"Still sounds risky."

"What else have we got? I've made no progress at all. I have to do something."

"Ok, I'll get the pass. You wait here."

She disappeared down the tunnel. I ate more while I waited. I looked back at my list of suspects. There was something odd about it, but I couldn't think what it was. Just something odd. I took another look at Weinberg's papers, then shoved them in my inside coat pocket for safe keeping.

Josie came back and handed me the pass. "Your best way in is through that kitchen. I'll take you there. I also got a list of where these people are likely to be found."

"Thanks kid, you think of everything."

"Someone has to."

I didn't take the bait. I'd been down that road with Josie before, and ended up on the losing end every time. She lead me to the kitchen and I could see what she meant. A large steel counter spanned most of the room, and stood between the ceiling camera and the vent. I popped open the grate, crawled through, worked my way over to the door, then opened it and acted as though I was walking in. I flipped on the light, looked around, then flipped it back off and walked out, into a long hallway.

After walking around I got my bearings. I'd been in this section, although it wasn't where I'd worked. I pulled out the Plexol chip, clicked on its portable screen, and ran down my list. Sal would be a few floors up. I took the escalator since that's where a lot of the coders gathered and I thought I might run into a few former co-workers that way. But they were all new faces.

I found Sal's office, a small glass enclosed cube, but he wasn't there. I glanced over at his screen but there was nothing of interest on it. I wandered around asking people if they'd seen him, and finally spotted him chewing out a coder sitting in a cubicle, looking miserable.

"I told you before, the point isn't just to spew out code as fast as possible. It has to actually work."

"It does work, there's just a small glitch in the—"

"The whole thing is one big glitch. Start over. Think it through this time. Give me something to work with here."

Sal glanced up as I approached. There was a moment of confusion, then he smiled. "Quint, what the hell?"

"Hey Sal, just stopping by to visit."

"These guys aren't allowed visitors, I barely give them

bathroom breaks."

"But it's you I'm visiting."

"Oh, well why didn't you say so. Let's go back to my office. They bumped me up to project manager. Remember when Joth was managing us? You thought he was an asshole, you should see me when I get worked up."

"I think I just did."

"What, that? That was nothing. Come on in, have a seat. Where've you been keeping yourself?"

"Drifting around mostly."

"Oh. Wasting time. You were always a good coder, Quint, but I could tell the pressure was too much for you."

"Well, at a certain point I guess I decided it wasn't for me."

"You dropped out is what you did. You failed. You should have stuck around. Look at me. My own office. The only downside is I'm not coding anymore. I miss it."

"Well, you must have a few projects going on the side. Just to keep your hand in it."

"Not really."

"Nothing?"

"I just told you. No."

There was an awkward silence. I decided to change gears. "So, do they have you doing any work on the brain chip? I hear it's pretty interesting."

"No, they've got me mostly on search and ad integration. I suppose they'll port anything I do over to the brain chip project since that's their current darling. A lot of money flowing around that division. If you're trying to get back in the door, that's where you want to be."

"It's an idea I've been kicking around."

"You'd have to catch up with these teenagers they've been hiring. But you've got the skills, no doubt about that. A little thin skinned, but no one's perfect."

"I guess not. Well, I don't want to use up more of your time. Just thought I'd stop by and say hi."

I stood up and shook his hand. "I'll see you around, Sal."

"Sure, stop by anytime, Quint. And if you get a gig over in brain chip, pull me over there."

"You've got it."

I wandered down the hall, taking a peek at my list. Sal had given me a good idea. I could use a feigned interest in rejoining the company as my excuse to have a quick chat with these people. Networking. I'd always hated the word in anything other than a digital context, but in this case it was the perfect cover.

Next up was Hamson Rilder, a large guy with big meaty hands that was working on treadmill and people mover software. Apparently there was an art to handling what they called a "fall down event." After Hamson was Tamera Quang. She was slim with a thin, lopsided smile, and tapped her nails on the edge of a view screen while talking to me. She was project manager on educational software and cyberverse integration, whatever the hell that means. Then came Billy "Blaze" Walker. I'd known Blaze back in my coding days. Back then he'd never impressed me much with his coding skills, but somehow he'd managed to rise through the ranks and was heading the automated toy division, overseeing IE for every imaginable kid friendly gadget, everything from teddy bears to starter computers.

Each person I talked with seemed engrossed in their work, and I knew from experience how Plexol could squeeze every last drop out of its workers. The more interviews I conducted, the more I became convinced that no one in middle management could be behind the brain chip virus. It was too huge an enterprise, too time consuming. The person we were looking for had either left Plexol, or was high enough in the ranks that they didn't have to account for their time.

I returned to the kitchen, faked leaving and shut off the lights, doubled back and snuck down into the vent. Josie was nowhere to be found. I uncovered the laptop and looked to see if it had recovered any other tidbits from the chip card. Nothing. I sifted through my options. I could shift gears and try to crack the virus, but Plexol already had people working that angle and they'd gotten nowhere. I could continue tracking down potential suspects, hoping to come face to face with the right person, and realize it. That was seeming hopeless as well. The chip card wasn't offering up any useful information. I needed a new angle. I needed to breathe new life into this investigation.

I pulled out the Plexol chip again and ran through the list, and it finally struck me what had bothered me before. While everyone on there matched the profile, none of them worked in the brain chip division. If this were an inside job, it would probably be someone there. A coder could look like they were working combating the virus, all the while actually preventing it from being removed. I'd just spent all day pretending I wanted to get into that division, it now seemed like doing so would be the best way to meet the major players and see what I could find out. It would also get me out of the damned vent.

Josie was still MIA, but I didn't have time to play maze hunt. I grabbed my gear, worked my way back to the kitchen, and wandered the hallways until I found Joth's office. He wasn't there so I made myself comfy. After 10 minutes of waiting I got antsy and started wandering around the work space. It was a real beehive, with the main hum coming from the giant room of coders. I walked around, looking over shoulders. Sal wasn't kidding, a lot of these people looked like they were fresh out of college, maybe younger. Or was I just getting older.

Across the room I spotted Joth, who saw me and put on a big fake smile, walking over as though he hadn't seen me in years. "Why Quint, good to see you. Why don't we go to my office and catch up."

"Sounds swell."

In his office the smile faded into a tight line beneath his nose. He spoke quietly so I had to lean forward to hear him. "Quint, what are you doing up here?"

"I guess I got tired of the gutter. I've got a new angle. I want you to hire me to work on the brain chip. That would give me access to the main players and a nice chunk of data to play with. This working underground thing is getting me nowhere. I'm too isolated from where the action is happening."

Joth scratched his cheek and looked off into space a moment. "I . . . don't know."

"Ok, what don't you know."

"It seems risky."

"Hide in plain sight, Joth. It makes sense. I've spent the day glad handing a bunch of project managers, now I come to you, my old boss, and you make me an offer I can't refuse. I'm a logical hire, I have experience, good coder, clean record."

"Look, I think this is a bad idea, but if you think it's the best approach we'll give it a try. But you can trust no one here. Do not let on about the investigation. Play it straight, figure out what you can. And for god's sake don't waste your time trying to crack the virus, I've already got an army working on that. I need you on task, not wandering off into a digital wonderland."

"Don't worry. Just give me a cube off in a corner where no one will bother me. Upgrade my access so I can poke around some useful databases. This is our best bet."

"I hope you're right. Now look, be careful what you say to these people. They know there's a virus, but that's all they know. The memory loss thing, that's not known and we need to keep it that way"

"Got it."

Joth sent me down to personnel to get set up, then stuck me in the cube farm, off in a corner, just like I'd asked him to. I introduced myself around, then got to work. First I hit the time log database to see if any of my fellow code monkeys had been cutting back on hours. Across the board, they had actually increased their time logged since the virus was first detected. Thanks to some nifty legislation Plexol had championed, none of these suckers were getting overtime, so that was just more free labor Plexol was raking in. Of course, the higher ups would always dangle a big fat carrot over everyone's head. That kept them in line. The ones that didn't burn out from the stress, that is.

The next rabbit hole I jumped down was a lookup that would show me what software was being run on which work stations. There are certain tools that would be of more value to someone protecting the virus than someone trying to eradicate it. This likewise revealed nothing, but there was one interesting glitch. A block of data that I didn't have access to. It looked to be a different division, but for some reason this data was on the same database as the brain chip division. I tried a few work arounds but couldn't get at it. I made a mental note to ask Joth about this data. It could just be health records or some other confidential info that required a higher access level. Still, it was a black box, and I enjoy looking inside black boxes.

I switched gears and looked over the work logs to see which coders had been most successful in removing the virus, even if it was only temporarily. One of them, Max Stigg turned out to be a few cubes down. I went to one of the ubiquitous coffee stations and loaded up my standard issue Plexol mug, then headed over to meet Max. He had long stringy hair and the glazed look of someone who stares at view screens all day. When I said "hi" he grunted a hello back without looking up. Ignoring newcomers was considered normal behavior in this environment, part of the Plexol hazing. What purpose it was meant to serve I never could tell. Only I wasn't really a newcomer. I had seniority over this stringy code slinger, he just didn't know it yet. I needed to change that.

"So I don't remember you from when I used to work over in Joth's old division."

That got him interested. He looked up. "When was that?"

"Oh, I while back. I've been on sabbatical. Nice to be back in the cube again. After all those years working here, it's good to be back at the keyboard."

"Yeah."

"How long you been here, uh . . ."

"Max. About a year."

"Oh, newbie. Well, you lasted your first year, you'll probably make it."

That took him down a notch. Now it was time to take him back up. Coders have fragile egos, which makes them that much easier to play.

"So Joth tells me you're one of his top guys."

"Joth said that?"

"Well, not directly, but that's the impression I got. You

know how Joth is."

"I haven't actually talked to the guy that much."

"Well, he can be a little obtuse. He did mention you've made some progress on the virus."

"This virus, it's a work of art."

"How so?"

"Whoever wrote this thing has it hooked all the way into the OS. You can't just clean it, you have to reinstall the system from scratch. Only somehow whoever launched this thing knows we've done that and they just reinstall the virus. They have to have some sort of feedback device."

"Well, the brain chip has broadcast capability. I suppose it latches onto that and sends out the warning when the wipe is initiated. Then all you'd have to do is send out a ping to see when the system is back up, and then inject the virus back in."

He mulled this over. "That all makes sense. The question is, how do you interrupt that cycle?"

"I suppose you could find the broadcast code that tells the black hat his virus is installed and running, then add that into your OS. Create a false ok signal. The black hat thinks his virus is up and running, but it's not. Just the fake signal."

"I like that. Is that the angle you're taking?"

"I'm still getting up to speed on the code, it'll be a while before I'm contributing anything useful."

"So you don't mind if I work on that? If it pans out I'd give you a share of the credit."

I knew from experience that a "share" of the credit usually meant a pat on the back as the guy who just ripped off your idea rode up the golden escalator without you, but I didn't give a crap. If this guy could make some progress on removing the virus, that was ok by me.

"Sure, no problem Max. Take a shot at it."

I started to walk off but he stopped me. "Hey, I didn't catch your name."

"Quint. Quint Heldin."

"Glad to meet you Quint. I'll let you know if I get anywhere with this."

I went back to my cube feeling good. If nothing else, maybe I'd set Max on the right course. It was odd that Joth as project manager hadn't thought of this approach, but he probably had a lot of other things going on at the same time.

I'd stuck my laptop in a drawer and pulled it out now to check on its progress. It had pulled a short fragment off the card, too short to be usable, but was working on finding more pieces. I made copies of everything to my Plexol chip, then shoved the laptop back into the drawer and got back to work. I pulled up a database that showed the time of each attempt to reinstall the OS. I then cross referenced this with a database that showed activity at each work station. I could see a bump at the time of the attempted reinstall. What I was interested in finding was a bump after that, something that would show activity at the time the virus was being sent to each brain chip. The bump showed up, but when I tried to tie it in to a specific workstation, I hit the same wall as before. The information I needed was in the database I couldn't access. This couldn't be a coincidence. Assuming this was an inside job, someone was making sure to cover his tracks. I set my workstation to the task of cracking into the secret database, then went off to find Joth in hopes he might have access to it.

Halfway to Joth's office, I saw him walking my way. He looked pissed.

"Quint, just the man I was coming to see. Join me in my office."

He doubled back and I chased after him. In his office he sat down, glaring at me.

"Please tell me it's a coincidence that you're on the floor all of 20 minutes and suddenly one of my top programmers is off task, working on something I did not assign him."

"If you mean Max, I'm guilty as charged. I just thought a new approach on the virus would—"

"Look Quint, I'm project manager, remember? If you were an actual normal employee I'd be showing you the door right now."

"I thought he was supposed to be working on removing the virus."

"He was. Last week. Now I have him on another project. Other people are assigned to the virus. Max already wasted too much time on that and I need him on more important things."

"What the hell is more important than removing the virus."

"You see, once again, that's something for the project

manager to decide. The *project manager*. Not . . ."

"What, a code monkey? Joth, I think you've forgotten what our objective is here. You brought me on for a specific purpose."

"Right, which was find the source, not take my workers off task. You're the one who forgot the objective. And as far as I can tell, you've made no progress towards it as a result."

"Well, that's where you're wrong. Twice now I've hit the same brick wall, and I think it might be what we're looking for. It's a database I don't have access to. I was hoping you did."

"I've already given you access to everything I can. If you hit an encrypted database, someone else is protecting it and I can't find out who or why."

"Well, then I just have to brute force it."

"So your best lead so far involves brute forcing an encrypted database on the Plexol server? Do you have any idea the level of encryption we have here? It could take about a billion years to decrypt that thing, and even then you're not sure what's inside. It might be nothing."

"You have the source code for the encryption algorithm?"

"I can get it, but I don't think that's going to move you one step closer."

"It might, it might not. But I think this database might be the key. It's worth devoting resources to."

"Fine, I'll get you the source code. I'll send it to your e-drop. Check it on the laptop, not the workstation."

"Ok." I got up to leave, but Joth grabbed my arm.

"Quint, I'm sorry for being impatient. There's a lot at stake here."

"Like what, your next promotion?"

"Don't be cynical, you know what I mean."

I left and went back to work. I pulled out the laptop and logged into my e-drop. The source code wasn't there yet, but there was a message. I opened it and realized it was from the homeless guy I'd given my dumpster rights to. It said:

"Hey man, I just saw that guy again. He wasn't all dressed up this time, but it was him. Just saw him walking around. Thought I'd let you know."

The timestamp indicated the message had been sent today, but that didn't make sense. Perhaps there was an error in the beta brain chips that screwed up the time code.

Suddenly the encryption source code appeared on the screen. Joth had come through. I opened it up and worked my way through it. There were definitely bits of code in there I had worked on. And while Joth was right—it could theoretically take a billion years to crack the encryption, I knew a few tricks he didn't, including a back door I routinely left in all my code. This, of course, was strictly against Plexol rules, but it had served me well in the past.

I downloaded a chunk of the encrypted database, then set up some programs locally to try to crack it open. Running this process locally would give me less processing power, but it meant no one on the network was likely to figure out what I was up to.

I pulled out the laptop and checked the progress. Nothing new. I stopped all running processes, copied over another chunk of the database from the work station, and set the laptop to work on that chunk, using some different tools from the work station and thereby improving my odds of getting results.

With all my computing resources locked up, I thought about disappearing back into the vent for a while and catching up with Josie. But I figured walking around meeting some more coders would be a better use of time. I talked to a few people who had spent a lot of time on killing the virus. The more I talked to them, the more clear it became that while they knew the software side, they didn't really understand the hardware side of the device. To my mind, you needed both, but I suppose it made sense that coders would focus on code. The other thing that struck me as odd is that none of them had actually attempted to decompile the virus itself. My workstation was already maxed out with decryption, so I opened a virtual session to be run off the server, loaded the virus in a sandbox, and then ran a decompiler on it. The virus itself was pretty small and decompiling it would be easy, especially running off the main frame, which could grab any unused cycles from the connected work stations and devote them to tasks on the fly. I made a backup copy of the virus to my Plexol chip, shoved it into my pocket, took a quick visit to the closest kitchenette, grabbed some food, and went back to watch the decompiler work its magic.

Little by little on the screen before me the code unravelled. It wasn't pure source code so I needed to tease it apart to make sense of it. Everything was chunked together in ways that made sense to a computer, not a person. As I worked through it, though, I began to see the logic at work. I opened a few drawers until I found a small e-sketch board. I drew a flow chart that represented the logic of the virus while I worked through the code. Piece by piece it revealed itself. There was also a little extra bit that didn't fit in with the code. It was 5 characters of plain text that had been stuck in as a comment. "Marea". What was Marea? The coder's girlfriend? The company? The coder's pseudonym? I did a lookup. Marea is Spanish for "tide". Why tide? What did that have to do with the brain chip?

I decided to leave this puzzle for later and went back to flowcharting the virus. At this point I had the whole thing decompiled and was scrolling around the chunks of code figuring out how it worked. One section in particular was of interest. It was a burst of random noise that could issue from the device. It seemed to come right after the subroutine that handled the advertising during the user's dream cycle. If the virus was taking over this function to insert its own message, then the burst could serve to somehow distract the mind, or perhaps it directly wipes the user's memory of having received the message. That could explain the memory loss people were suffering.

I worked through the remainder of the code, copied the flow chart to my laptop, and brought the e-sketch board up to Joth's office to show him what I'd found. He seemed annoyed that I was interrupting him again.

"Quint, you can't keep running up here all day. It looks weird. The other coders don't do that."

"Joth, I've got something good here. Take a look at the flow chart. See that burst? That could be the cause of the memory loss."

"So you're completely off task again."

"What the hell are you talking about, I may have found the cause of the problem."

"The cause of the problem is some coder holed up somewhere messing with our brain chip. I hired you to find him, which it's becoming more and more clear you aren't going to do. I guess it's my fault. Hire a coder to do a detective's job. I just thought with your background you'd come up with some way to figure out who was behind this. But all you seem interested in is code. It's getting us nowhere."

"You've really lost it. Right here is the code that's the likely cause of the memory loss. All we have to do is work out a block to that subroutine, insert it into the virus, and replace the existing virus with our new hybrid. That wouldn't trigger the warning system that lets the bad guys know we've tampered with their code, but it would hopefully stop the memory loss."

"That's a lot of maybes, Quint. I can't devote resources to some half cracked theory."

"Joth, it's worth a shot."

"Forget it. I'm sorry Quint. I made a mistake. I'm taking you off this job. I'll pay you for the time you've spent. I'm going to find someone else to work on this. Leave everything at your workstation the way it is. Just leave."

"Are you nuts? I'm finally getting close."

"You're getting close? Who is behind this? What's his name? Where is he?"

"You know what I mean."

"Yes, but you don't seem to understand what I'm saying. Quint, forget it. I'm sorry I got you involved. Go back to whatever you were doing before I signed you up for this operation. Forget it ever happened."

I couldn't believe what I was hearing, but there was no more point in arguing with Joth. As I walked out of his office he called out, "leave your stuff where it is, I'll take care of it. Just go."

I had hoped to at least grab the laptop, but that obviously wasn't in the chips. Joth had a couple Plexol gorillas following me down the hall, making sure I left without taking anything. Maybe stepping on his toes as project manager had really gotten under his skin. Or maybe I really had messed up the investigation, although it seemed like I was so close. If only he'd given me a little more time.

When I got outside I saw Josie sitting on a bench near the NanoRail station. She waved and I walked over. She had an odd look on her face.

"Tough break, Quint."

"I guess so. Want to go get a drink somewhere to celebrate?"

"I'd love to, but I'm assigned to a new job."

"That was fast."

"That's how it works, Quint."

"So, see you around sometime?"

"Sometime."

She got up and walked away. Part of me wanted to chase after her, but I'd made that mistake before. It just made her run faster. Watching her walk away was too painful, so I got up and headed for the NanoRail. I wasn't even thinking about where I was going when I realized I still had the Plexol chip in my pocket. I pulled it out and flipped on the attached view screen, looking for Max Stigg's address. It was one stop away and when I got there I left the NanoRail and walked around. He lived in one of those tall chrome buildings the coders all seem to gravitate to. Across the street was a friendly looking tavern called GIGO that already had a crowd building as people left work either for a drink before they head home or a quick pick-me-up before they head back to work in their cube. I grabbed a bar stool near the window and kept an eye on Max's place. I had no idea if or when he'd be coming home tonight, so I decided I'd better start with coffee instead of the hard stuff.

The place was filling up and the louder the crowd got, the more they turned up the music. It was modern stuff, not my style. I was never much good at waiting, and waiting in this environment was starting to get on my nerves. I was about to leave when I spotted a cute redhead in her 20's giving me the eye. She was pure curves and magic, with black boots, a short skirt, and a smile that looked like trouble. I was still stinging from the way Josie had just disappeared back into the ether, and it felt good to be noticed. I smiled back. She smiled wider. I knew I should walk over, but I didn't want to leave my post by the window. I looked out again to see if there was any sign of Max. When I turned back, the redhead was standing next to me.

"I saw you today."

"Oh yeah? You must have been flippin' through the fashion magazines."

She laughed. "Yeah, something like that. I work at Plexol. Brain chip division. I saw you talking to Max."

"You know Max?"

"I know everyone."

"I see, so now it's my turn to get known"

"Something like that."

I took another look out the window. While I was all in favor of female companionship, this girl was going to mess up my stakeout. I needed to shake her. In a friendly way. Not really my specialty.

"Well, I was just about to leave, but maybe we'll bump into each other, um . . ."

"Heather."

"Ok then Heather." I held out my hand for her to shake but she left it hanging there between us.

"I hear you got canned today."

"Word spreads fast."

"I talked to Max, he said you were a smart guy, lots of experience. Just started back, then they fire you. That doesn't make sense."

"Ok, so it doesn't make sense."

"I poked around your workstation before they came to clean it out. I noticed you left your laptop. It wasn't a Plexol laptop so I figured it was yours."

"And where is it now?"

"I've got it."

"I don't suppose you'd like to give it back to me."

"I might. Depends."

"On . . ."

"Let's go somewhere we can talk."

"Where to?"

"Max's place is right across the street. I've got the key. We can talk there."

"So you and Max are . . . friends?"

"Something like that."

Sitting in Max's apartment and waiting for him there sounded about 1,001 times better than sitting here bombarded by bad music and loud laughter.

Heather and I dashed across the street and she took me inside. The building had a huge lobby with a holographic fountain. I'd seen them before. If you looked close, each fake drop of water had in image in it. Combined they would form one large image, constantly shifting and moving. They would usually just form patterns and abstract shapes, but this one was creating faces of famous tech gurus from the past. This truly was a coder's paradise.

The elevator was glass and fast. My ears popped on the way up. Heather led me down the hallway and I couldn't help noticing the nice way she moved when she walked. It was no Josie walk, but it would do in a pinch. She turned back and caught me staring.

"So, you like redheads?"

"I'm partial to brunettes, but I got nothing against 'em."

"My natural color is brown, but I like to change it from time to time. It was blue with black streaks for a while."

"I think I changed the part in my hair once for about five minutes. It was traumatizing."

She laughed. We got to Max's door and she swiped a key chip. The door slid open with a whooshing sound and we walked in. The apartment was small but nice. Chrome and glass, sparse furniture. Gear in various states of disassembly covered one table. I examined a few pieces. It was old stuff, the type of thing I could happily spend hours playing around with. I was starting to like Max even more.

Heather was mixing a couple drinks and brought me one. "Have a seat," she said, gesturing to a small couch against the wall.

"About my laptop . . ."

"Don't be a bore. Let's talk first. Anyway, it's at my place so you'll have to wait to get it. Sit down."

I sat on one end of the couch and Heather sat dangerously close to me. I could smell her perfume. It wasn't the acrid synthetic stuff girls her age usually wore. She'd either dug up a cache of the old stuff or mixed her own. I took a swig of my drink. It was good and strong. This girl was starting to win points with me. She clinked her glass against mine and said, "here's to new friends."

"Here's to your drink mixing skills, kid."

"Glad you like it. So tell me, how did you manage to piss off Joth so fast that he had you out the door a few hours after you started?"

"I guess I was stepping on his toes when I got Max working on the virus again. I didn't realize he had been moved to another project."

"A lot of us were. It felt like people were finally making a little progress when they announced a new priority and shifted most of us over. There's basically just a skeleton crew working on the virus now."

"That so?"

"Yeah. Max was pretty psyched when you showed up. He figured maybe they were shifting back to the virus project. When he heard you got the boot he was pretty upset. Then Joth stopped by his cube and told him to get back to what he was working on and leave the virus project alone."

"Maybe Joth has other people working on the virus that you don't know about."

"Why do you say that?"

"On my journey through the main frame I kept bumping into an encrypted database. I have to wonder if he's got another

team stashed somewhere secretly working on the virus while he keeps his regular team on more profitable ventures."

"Could be. Is that really what you think?"

"I don't know what I think anymore, Heather. I was hoping to talk to Max and get some direction from him. Since Joth tossed me out the door I've been feeling like someone switched off my GPS."

"Well, he won't be here for a while, he works late. Why don't we head over to my place and you can get your laptop."

"I like that plan."

"I figured you would."

As I started to get up from the couch, she yanked me back down. "Just one more thing before we do that."

"Yeah?"

"What exactly were you working on?"

"Heather, I can't give you all the details."

"It's about the digital dementia, isn't it?"

"Um, how do you know about that?"

"I bought my mom a Plexol brain chip for her birthday last year. When she started having memory problems, I wondered if it had anything to do with the chip. When they told us about the virus, I put 10 and 10 together."

"Does your mother still . . ."

"She got the chip removed, but she's still having the memory problems. At least they haven't worsened since then, but still. She's only in her 50s. She should not be having memory loss at her age."

"I'm . . . sorry."

"A group of us have been working together to try to gather information. After hours, outside of Plexol. We know there are things they aren't telling us. I'm guessing you've got information that could help."

"Some. I wish I had more."

"You share what you've got, I share what I've got, and we see where it gets us."

"I'm ok with that. But first let's get my laptop."

"Fair enough."

She got up and walked to the door. I followed her out and down the hall to the next apartment. She opened the door with a key chip and we walked in. Her place looked pretty much like Max's, just a little more girled up.

"So, you live next door to Max?"

"Yeah, we're close. I've known him since we were born."

"Since you were born?"

"We're twins."

"I guess I hadn't noticed the resemblance."

"Take a look," she said, pointing to a picture of two kids on the wall. The resemblance between them was obvious.

"I guess the red hair threw me off."

"That's what it's supposed to do. Throw men off. Have a seat."

She gestured toward a loveseat that matched the one in

Max's place. I had a seat while she disappeared into her bedroom. A minute later she came out with black hair and my laptop in her hand. Both of these facts caught my interest in about equal measures. She smiled.

"There, you said you like brunettes better, but the closest I have is this black wig. What do you think."

"I think you'd look good with no hair."

"Hm. Not a bad idea."

"I wasn't suggesting it."

"Here's your laptop. I left it running."

I took a look to see if any progress had been made on either the chip card or the encrypted database. The chip card had been thoroughly searched and nothing new turned up. It was a lost cause. The encrypted database however was showing signs of progress. Potential progress anyway. The software had quickly rejected about a million possible approaches, which narrowed down the number of branches it would have to explore to hit the right one. I set the laptop on a table, then watched Heather push a button on a media card. Music came blasting from ceiling speakers.

"Oops, sorry," she yelled out. She fussed with the media card and the volume came down to a tolerable level.

I asked her, "should we be getting back to Max's place in case he comes home?"

"He'll buzz me when he gets back. Let's wait here. It's more comfortable."

She sat me back down on the loveseat and squeezed in next

to me. I couldn't help commenting this time, "You seem to like sitting close to me."

"Maybe I do. Does it bother you?"

"Not really. I'm just not sure how to take it."

"Don't over think it."

"I'll try to remember that."

"So I kept up my end of the bargain. Tell me what you know about the brain chip."

"I've got papers that explain a lot about the hardware, something you people seem to have neglected to look into."

I handed her Dr. Weinberg's papers, which she took as though it were an artifact from an ancient tomb. "Where on earth did you get this?"

"I got it."

"And you didn't bother to scan it?"

"I've been busy."

"Mind if I do?"

"Go for it."

She held the papers out in front of her and flipped through them quickly, then set them down. "There. You want a copy?"

"I thought you were going to scan those."

"I just did. Scan chip. I got it last year when I took my mom for the brain chip. They were on sale."

"I didn't even realize those were beyond prototype. Good god I've been out too long."

"I guess so if you're carrying around paper." She pulled a

Plexol chip out of her pocket, held it next to her temple, stared off into space a moment, then handed me the chip. "Here, copy off this, I need it back."

I made a copy onto my own Plexol chip, then handed hers back. She was staring off into space again.

"What are you doing?"

"I'm looking at the papers I just scanned."

"You can see them?"

"Of course. It's like they're right in front of me."

"That's amazing. So why not use that capability instead of a monitor at work?"

"That would mean giving Plexol access to my scan chip. I don't trust them."

"I'm right there with you."

She went quiet and stared off into space again. I got up and took a look at my laptop, then walked around a little. I found another media chip and used it to turn down the volume on the music. Heather didn't seem to notice, she was completely focused on the phantom image of the papers before her. Occasionally the tip of her tongue would come out from between her lips, then hide back inside. With the black wig on she looked just a little like Josie, except without that sad look in the eyes. It was that sad look that sucked me in every time.

Heather got up and walked toward me, stopping about an inch from my face. "Getting board, Quint?"

"I was."

"I don't want to be a bad host."

"I've got no complaints."

"Well, I'll look at the rest of that later. I agree, understanding the hardware is helpful. Let's talk more about what you know."

I sat down and she snugged in next to me. "I'm not making you nervous am I?"

"Not at all. But do me a favor."

"Anything."

"Take off the wig."

She laughed and pulled the wig off, throwing it on the table next to the laptop. "How's that?"

"Swell. So here's the good stuff. I'm fairly convinced it's an inside job, and I think whoever is working on it is using that encrypted database. At minimum they have someone inside to help them avoid any counter measures Plexol takes. They've also got people on the outside. They had some guy named Kett keeping an eye on me but I don't think he'll be bothering me anymore. The chip card I've been trying to crack was his. It broadcast to a car somewhere. At least I think it did."

She gave me a look I hadn't seen out of her pretty face before. Something like bewildered concern. "That's it?"

"Pretty much."

"Quint, that's crap."

"Thanks."

"I'm not kidding, you must be holding something back."

"Nothing useful."

She looked down, then back at me. Her eyes were welling up. "Then we really are no closer. That lead you gave Max, that was helpful. The rest of this stuff though . . ."

"You have to understand Heather, I wasn't working on cracking the virus, I was working on finding out who was behind it."

"Who had you working on that?"

"I've probably already told you more than I should. Let's just say it was someone at Plexol."

"Joth."

"I didn't say it was Joth."

"I know, I did. And you didn't say I was wrong. But if Joth is so concerned about finding the source, why not keep us working on virus removal? It doesn't make sense. And why pull you off the job?"

"I guess he was as unimpressed with my progress as you were."

She looked down again and I could see a single drop slowly travel down her cheek. I put my arm around her. "You're thinking about your mother, aren't you?"

"Yeah."

"Look kid, we'll work together on this. We'll figure something out."

"Quint, other than me and Max we only have 3 other people on this. And we've gotten nothing accomplished. I just don't think we'll ever . . ."

The tears came on like a sprinkler in Spring. She buried her head in my neck and I could feel the hot wetness on her face. I held her close. She felt good like that, although it made me feel guilty to think it. I guess I've got a weakness for sad women. Probably not the best thing to be attracted to, but no one really gets to decide what fires up their circuits. It's all hard wired from the time we're kids.

I could have sat there holding her for a good long time, but there was a buzz and then the click of the lock in the door opening. The door slipped open and in walked Max. He stopped about halfway through when he saw us huddled on the loveseat, and was about to back out when Heather called out, "it's ok Max, come on in. We need to talk."

He came in, grabbed a chair and sat across from us. She looked at him and he reached out to wipe the tears off her face with his sleeve. "What's going on here?"

"It's just me having one of my little breakdowns. Quint doesn't really have much info that can help us."

"Well, if we get inside that database . . ." I said, gesturing to my laptop.

"That could take years," she said, reminding me of Josie.

"Yeah, or it could take minutes," I said. "Come on kid, don't give up hope. Let's put our heads together and see what we can figure out."

Max walked over to look at the laptop, then turned back to

me. "So, what about the girl?"

"What girl," I asked.

"I saw a girl in Joth's office. Cute. Dark hair. Dark eyes. I was going up there to ask him to let me work late on the idea you gave me, but they were having some sort of intense discussion, so I left it alone."

"Wait, you saw her there after I was gone?"

"Yeah."

"But, that had to be Josie. She left when I did."

"Well, she must have come back. I'd never seen her before, so I figured it had to be connected to you somehow."

"She was working with me, but I guess Joth has her working on something else. But that's weird she came back after I left. I'm not sure what it means."

"It's just one more puzzle piece. Add it to the pile." Max got up and walked over to a console. He sat down and logged on to Plexol's system. He called over his shoulder, "come here you two, I want to show you something."

Heather and I walked over. Max pulled up the database I had been working on. He then pulled up the encryption header. "It's been changed," he said. "They added a new layer of encryption. Someone figured out what you were up to, Quint."

"Too late, I already grabbed a huge chunk and copied it to my laptop."

"Here's something else. Look at this." He pulled up the home screen for his virus eradication project. A grey box popped up, covering the screen. It said, "Project Cancelled." Max looked at me. "What do you make of that?"

"Joth is just making sure you stay on task?"

"I checked with three other people who had previously been on this project. They all hit the same wall."

"Ok, so what's it all add up to?"

"What if it's Joth? What if he's the one behind this?"

"I don't know Max. He's the one that hired me to work on this in the first place. Why would he bother pulling me out of the mothballs, it would only increase the odds of him getting caught."

"He came looking for you?"

"Well, come to think of it, I came looking for him. But he said he'd been searching for me. But now that you mention it, that doesn't add up. There were no messages from him in my e-drop. Maybe when I turned up he was afraid I already knew about the brain chip and was coming after him. Maybe he decided to keep his enemy close, send me down some blind alleys. But that's crazy. I've known Joth for years."

"People have a way of changing the longer they work there."

"Ain't that the truth. I'll have to ponder that one. What if Joth is Marea?"

"Marea?!" the twins said in unison.

"Yeah, that's the name I found in the virus when I decompiled it. I figured it must be someone's pseudonym. That's one theory anyway."

Heather looked at Max. "Do you want to tell him or should I?"

"Go ahead."

She turned to me. "The first time we rewrote the OS to the brain chips, we saw that the virus was reinstalled over it. We had a test chip set up in a room off the computer lab and we were monitoring all input and output. Right after the virus was successfully installed the chip broadcast a message in plain text. 'Marea.' After that they must have changed the code because all the subsequent transmissions were encrypted."

This got my interest. "Did you compare the later transmissions to each other?"

"Of course," said Max. "Our hope was they would be the same each time, so then we could use that as a way to crack the encryption, since we already knew the encrypted message was 'Marea.' But it was different each time. We still took a shot at it, but couldn't find a pattern."

"You still have these messages saved?"

"Of course."

"Copy them to my laptop and let me take a crack at them."

Max copied them over and I stole some processor cycles from the database decryption, assigning them to manipulating the Marea messages. My hunch was that the same message was being sent each time the virus was successfully reinstalled, but the encryption was changed slightly each time. Even with the variation, it would give me several samples of encrypted messages I could compare back to the original plain text.

I ran a few different programs, each plotting a different course to my goal. It was slow going so I completely shut down the database crack. Max and Heather were watching over my shoulder. Heather said, "You need something more powerful to crack that."

"This pup has more under the hood than you'd think. Just let me do my thing."

Heather drifted back to the love seat but Max stayed put, watching me work. Occasionally he'd point to a block of code he found interesting and I'd zero in on it to see what we could learn. I switched between programs to check the status of each attack. One of these worked by repeatedly encrypting the word "Marea" using different algorithms and based on increasingly complex prime numbers, hoping to arrive at an encrypted message that matched one of the messages we had intercepted. I got up and let Max play around with it a while. He seemed entranced.

"Where did you get all this software? It's perfect for this."

"I've got a good supplier, he always keeps a few laptops under wraps, fully loaded like this."

"I've got to get one of those."

"I might be able to hook you up. They're pricey. It's a black market item and he takes some risk having it around."

"And you left it just sitting out at Plexol?"

"I wasn't given much choice. It was straight from Joth's office to the exit."

"That's odd, he wouldn't even let you get your own laptop?"

"I guess you think that supports your theory, but it could just be his way of being a jerk."

Max turned his attention back to the screen, and I sat down next to Heather. She was staring off into space again. Without looking at me she said, "this thing is pretty amazing. Originally, the internal broadcast function was only intended to communicate the contents of whatever information was being sought on the cyberverse. This could be done through audio, visual, or both. There was even a tactile function that was being beta tested but was left out of the final version. Too bad, that really opens up some possibilities."

"So then Plexol piggy backed on the audio visual function to do the advertising."

"Dreamvertising. That was the internal name for it anyway. It took some clever coding but yeah, they took over the internal broadcast mechanism for that."

"Ok, so where did the memory wipe function come from? Why would that be in there in the first place?"

"That's just it, there was no device specifically intended for that purpose. So whoever wrote the virus had to re-purpose some other part of the chip. My guess is they use a managed frequency pulse from the audio broadcast to create some sort of brain wave disturbance. At sufficient amplitude it could create permanent damage to surrounding neurons and synapse receptors."

"But why bother?"

"They must be broadcasting something instead of the

dreamvertising that they don't want the user to consciously remember. The memory loss would cover up the receipt of the message, but if properly handled, would leave the effect of the message in place. Some sort of command that the user follows without remembering why."

"Plausible. It would be awfully nice to intercept one of those messages, see what's being plugged into people's brains."

Heather turned and looked at me.

"Sorry, Heather, this has to be hard for you," I said.

"It's not that Quint, it's what you said about intercepting the message. We have. They're all encrypted, just like the post-virus installation message. Assuming the same code is being used to encrypt both messages, if we manage to crack 'Marea', we could potentially crack some of the messages too."

"That's good thinking kid."

We both looked over at Max. He must have felt the two sets of eyes on his back. Either that or the twins were doing that ESP thing. He called over his shoulder, "we're getting there. I give it a half hour before one of these programs cracks it open. It's a nice short message, just 5 characters. Non-trivial, but doable."

I turned back to Heather but she had that lost in space look on her face again. I was starting to feel useless. I pulled the Plexol chip from my pocket and pulled up the original list of suspects again. As I scrolled through them, I realized what had bugged me before. Joth's name wasn't on the list, even though he obviously matched the original profile. Had he intentionally left his name off?

Max called over his shoulder, "I was wrong. It took less than half an hour."

Heather and I jumped up and looked at the screen. There were 30 short lines of code. Those 30 lines represented the encryption algorithm for the 'Marea' message. Max pulled a chip out of his pocket and copied some data onto the laptop. "These are the messages we intercepted. I'm going to run a dictionary attack, encrypting every word in the dictionary with this algorithm. Then we'll compare the results to what's in the intercepted messages, find any matches, and then decode the message."

As he talked he set it all in motion. The dictionary attack was a classic approach, and depending on what you used as the word list it could be very effective. I asked Max, "how many words are in the dictionary you're using?"

"You had a good one on here, but I added a Spanish word list to it."

"Spanish. Why?"

"The brain chip has a basic translator built in, so it would automatically translate Spanish to English. From the user's perspective it would be the same. But from the sender's perspective it would add one more layer of obscurity, since anyone doing the dictionary attack we're doing is likely to just search English words and variants."

"Ok, but then why not add every known language?"

"Marea. It's a Spanish word. I figured maybe that was just a coincidence, but it won't hurt to try some other Spanish words and see what we find."

"That's right. Tide."

I mulled this over. What does the word "tide" have to do with a virus on a brain chip. I made a mental list of everything I knew about tides. They come in and go out. They leave things behind, laying in the sand. They can be affected by the gravity of the moon. Suddenly, it clicked. I pulled the chip card from my laptop and showed it to Max.

"Notice anything?"

"What's that symbol?"

"A crescent and a wave. The moon affects the tides. Marea. Maybe there's a connection."

"Where did you get that chip?"

"Off this hired pain-in-the-rump called Kett. He was tracking me for a while. He was using this card to communicate with whoever hired him, which seems to be the same person or people who are behind the virus."

"So maybe Marea is the organization."

"Or the pseudonym of the boss."

Heather came over to watch our progress on the dictionary attack. "Anything?"

"Not yet," Max said, "but I think we're on the right track here. Still, it's probably going to take a while. There's over 1,000,000 words and variants it has to encrypt and search for."

"On top of that," I added, "it's highly unlikely we'll find an exact match. There's likely another layer of encryption to help prevent the type of attack we're trying. But the software will also search for patterns using the encrypted word base as a source. That adds to the likelihood of success considerably, but also adds considerable time."

"Ok," she said, "Well, I've read as much about the brain chip as I can process for now. I need some air. Who's in the mood for a walk?"

She was looking straight at me. Max called over his shoulder, "I'm staying here. You guys go. If anything pops up I'll send a ping to Heather's com chip."

Heather grabbed a jacket, grabbed my hand, and pulled me out the door. We took the elevator down and were soon out on the street. It was dark out and the air was crisp. There were a lot of other people out and there was a celebratory vibe. Heather took my arm and we walked along, catching snippets of conversations, watching people popping in and out of bars. We reached a small park and she led me to a bench where we sat down. She kept hold of my arm. I turned to her.

"So Heather, are you this friendly with everyone you meet?"

"I like you Quint. You remind me of a guy I knew."

"Well, that's a recipe for disaster."

"How's that?"

"Whoever he was, I'm not him."

"Ok, then tell me who you are."

"I'm just a burnt out coder. I was like your brother when I

was his age. I did my time at Plexol. But the years rolled by and there I was, still stuck in the cube farm. I never did play the political game well. I just figured, someone would notice I was a damned good coder and promote me. Well, they noticed I was a good coder and decided to keep me right where I was."

"So what did you do after you left?"

"Travel. Spend some of the hard earned credits I'd saved up. Then these past 6 months I've been mostly drifting, trying to live outside society."

"Why?"

"There was some point I was trying to prove. To tell you the truth, I'm not really sure what it was anymore. I guess prove I could be self-sufficient. Prove I didn't need anyone."

"So someone broke your heart."

"Ok, that's enough probing. I still don't understand why you warmed to me so quickly."

"I guess I'm that way. If I like someone, I like them. I'm pretty decisive in that way. Of course, I've made my share of mistakes. But my instinct is usually right."

"So what's your instinct tell you about me?"

"You've been hurt. You took your show on the road hoping to leave the hurt behind, and probably found out everywhere you went it was right there waiting for you."

"That's not bad, kid. You may be a little psychic."

"Quint, I've been hurt too. We all have. I guess sometimes it just goes a little deeper."

"That's the truth."

"But I also think you're ready to return."

"To what?"

"Life. The world. I don't know. Maybe you're ready to love again."

I mulled that one over. Mulled over everything she'd said. Was I a fool to trust her, or a fool not to? That's the problem, you never can be sure.

Heather stood up. "Come on, there's someone I want you to meet."

A short walk later we were at yet another apartment building that seemed to have been designed for the many coders who live in this neighborhood. Upstairs she introduced me to a heavyset man wearing a wrist computer. These had gone out of fashion about 10 years ago, but so had his long side burns.

"Quint, this is Milos. He works at Plexol too. Brain chip division."

I shook his hand. "Glad to meet you Milos. I'm surprised we didn't meet today at Plexol during my brief if less than stellar return."

"Oh, I've been working from home a lot lately."

"Really, I didn't know they allowed that."

"Joth has been pretty accommodating."

"Hm. Awfully nice of him."

Heather pulled me over to a couch where we sat while Milos stood awkwardly staring at us. "Sit down, Milos, let's talk."

"Oh, yes, of course."

He pulled up a chair. "So what brings you two here?"

"Quint is helping us with the brain chip problem." She turned to me. "Milos has been working on it too, in his spare time."

"Yes, well, I seem to have less and less of that all the time. They keep me pretty busy."

Something occurred to me then. "Milos, I'm curious. When you work from home, do they have you log in to the same time log system as the one they have on site?"

He looked confused for a moment. "Um, I'm not sure what you mean."

"You know, are you logged in to the same database, or do they keep that time log separate?"

"I'm not sure. I guess you'd have to ask Joth that."

"Hm. Not likely."

Heather gave me a "what on earth are you talking about" look, then changed the topic. "So Milos, what do they have you working on?"

"I'm doing a comparative study of which advertising is more effective in the brain chip context, so we can maximize value for the advertisers."

"How?"

"We track sales of products bought by brain chip users, who are divvied up into categories dependent on the type, number, and duration of ads they are receiving."

"But how would you know what they bought?"

"They fill out a survey every so often."

"Hm. Interesting."

We sat through another awkward silence, then Heather jumped up. "Well, I can see we've interrupted you, I just wanted you to meet Quint. You'll be at the next meeting, right?"

"Of course, Heather. I'll see you there."

Once we were back out on the street Heather leaned in to me. "Sorry about that Quint, I don't know why he was acting so weird."

"I have a hunch."

"I know, you're going to say he was jealous or something."

"Actually, no."

"And why were you asking him about the time log?"

"Heather, somewhere there's a secret army of coders working on the virus. What better way to manage them than by having them work from home, separate from each other so they only know each other by their work, not their identity. They log in to the encrypted database so their existence is invisible to the Plexol management."

"Are you saying Milos is working for Marea?"

"I don't know. I'm just saying it's a possibility. Certainly, having him keep apprised of the progress you and the others are making on defeating the virus would be a priority for Marea. It does all sort of fit together."

"But Quint, I've known Milos for a long time. We went to school together."

"I knew lots of good people who once they got sucked into the Plexol machine became suddenly very different. Greed and the lust for power can change people, Heather."

"He was acting strange, but I refuse to believe he'd be involved in something like that."

"You can believe what you like. The possibility is still something we need to accept."

Heather pulled out her com chip. It was vibrating and on the tiny screen there was a message. "Max says to come back, he's found something."

We walked quickly and were soon huddled around the console in Heather's apartment. Max pointed to a line of code.

"It's not plain text yet, but you see the patterns here?"

"I see what appear to be patterns, but I've been fooled before. Let me sit down a second."

I opened a new program and ran some tests on the string of characters that had caught his interest. "There's a decent probability that that's a pseudo random string."

"Ok, so how do we test it?" He asked.

I opened another program, this one designed for pattern recognition and comparison. I grabbed the string of code along with several other lines nearby and fed them into the software. I explained, "it will run several different analyses of the code, then compare results. In essence it's a dictionary attack using patterns rather than words. It generates the patterns on the fly rather than using a predetermined list like we used in the dictionary attack.

The patterns it generates will be mutations of the patterns it detects in the code. It then pairs them and subtracts one from the other to see what's left. You know it would be nice to have another laptop to run this one, we're really running out of processing power here."

"Let's make that a priority. You mentioned hooking me up with your supplier."

"I've got a better plan. Transfer the credits to me, I'll go pick one up for you tomorrow."

"So you don't trust me."

"Don't take it personally, I just met you today."

"I don't take it personally. I take it as a good sign. Here's a credit chip. Take what you need."

Heather looked surprised. "Max, if he doesn't trust you, why are you trusting him?"

"I'm trusting him with credits. I can always make those back. It's different from trusting me with his contact. Someone could end up in jail."

"I guess that makes sense. You know, we went to visit Milos, and Quint thinks he's working for the black hats, for Marea."

"I've pondered the same thing."

"What? Why didn't you say something?"

"Heather, it's just a theory. I knew it would upset you, which apparently it has, so I kept it to myself. I did, however, feed him a little misinformation, just to see where it turns up."

"What did you tell him?"

"My dear, if I told you that it would spoil the experiment."

"Oh, so now you don't trust me?"

"That's not what I said, and don't start a fight with me. We need to stay focused here. Quint, I'm going to devote 30% resources to the pattern attack for now, the rest to decrypting the messages. I don't think we're going to be seeing any results for a while, so I'm going to turn in."

He got up and kissed his sister on the forehead. "I trust you completely, Heather. Don't get upset."

He turned to me. "If anything turns up on the laptop, wake me up."

"What makes you think I'll be here?"

He just smiled and left. I looked at Heather. "What's he know that I don't."

"He knows I usually get what I want."

"And how does he know what you want?"

"I haven't exactly been subtle, have I?"

"I guess not. I still don't really understand . . ."

"Don't over think it."

"I think I heard that somewhere before."

"Are you tired?"

"Why?"

"Just wondering. I stay up late. Not everyone does."

"I'm fine."

"You like holofilms?"

"Some. I like the old ones."

"Why doesn't that surprise me. Let me guess, you like the old 2Ds."

"Some. There was some good stuff back then. But I suppose there must be some newer stuff that's not all bad."

She leaned closer. "Oh yeah? Like what?"

I looked into her eyes and saw so many things there. Behind her boldness was a vulnerability, a longing to be loved. It pulled me closer and without thinking I was kissing her. I ran my hand up the back of her neck and grabbed her hair, pulling her back onto the love seat as we continued kissing. My other hand went exploring, making journeys all over her body, then returning to my favorite spots and exploring deeper. Her body felt good beneath me. After the possibilities of the small love seat were exhausted, I picked her up and carried her into her bedroom, throwing her on the bed. I stood looking at her. So beautiful. There's nothing any artist in this world can create more beautiful than a woman's body. I lay down beside her and picked up where we'd left off. Soon our clothes were on the floor and we were entwined, her skin warm and soft against mine. Hours went by like that, and when we were done she wrapped around me, head on my chest, and we fell asleep.

6.

When I woke up I could hear her in the kitchen. I stretched, got up, and peaked out the door. She heard me and looked back, giving me a smile I was starting to like more and more.

"I'm making breakfast."

"Sounds good to me. I'm gonna jump in the shower."

"Well be quick, it's almost done."

I cleaned up, got dressed, and sat down with her to a solid breakfast.

"This is good Heather."

"Glad you like it."

"I like you too."

"That's good Quint, because I don't want that to be a 1 night stand."

"Kid, you still don't really know me. I might get on your nerves once you do."

"Stick around long enough for me to find out."

I finished my food and leaned back in my chair, just looking at her. Then the door buzzed, slid open, and in walked Max. "So, any progress?"

Heather and I looked at each other and smiled. Max made an exasperated sound.

"I don't mean that type of progress. The laptop."

He walked over to see for himself, while we sat there like a couple of happy idiots. He punched a few keys, then looked over at us. "If you 2 could come back to earth for a few minutes, you might want to take a look at this.

The messages were decoded. As I read through them I could see they were all directions to the user to buy a specific product, at a specific store, at a specific time. I looked at Heather.

"Remember what Milos was saying? This is a natural extension of that. Instead of straight dreamvertising, they are giving a direct command to the user's brain. Then they track compliance."

"Ok, but with what objective? To sell a few more bars of soap?"

"It has to be a beta test for something bigger. I suppose on a mass scale, once you perfected this you would sell buyers to sellers. You've got 1,000 widgets to sell? Great. I've got 1,000 people who I can make buy your widget. Pay me a percentage and we're good to go."

"And what about the memory loss?"

"The user would be consciously aware of a direct command and his mind would naturally rebel. I'm thinking that the intent isn't so much to wipe the memory as to interfere with that portion of the brain that analyses the command. Remove that and you have compliance. Perhaps memory loss is just a side effect."

Max looked at Heather. "This still gets us no closer to helping mom."

"Or anyone else, since we still don't know how to stop this."

I thought this over. "You know, there is a way. If we go to the press . . ."

Heather grabbed a stray strand of hair and twirled it between her fingers. "We've discussed that. Our whole group. Come to think of it, Milos was the one who talked us out of it. His reasoning was that this was probably an outside job, and the intent was to create a scandal that would bring down Plexol. At the time it made sense, but as time has passed I realize how foolish we've been to stay quiet."

"Well, there's no point in you two losing your jobs," I said. "I'll go talk to a buddy of mine who works for Holo-News 10. He's not a reporter, just a programmer, but he can vouch for me and hook me up with the right people."

The twins agreed. I gave Heather a long hug, a kiss goodbye, and I was back outside on my way to the NanoRail. About halfway there a black van pulled up next to me. The door slid open, and out jumped the person I least expected to see in the whole world.

"Kett?"

"Hello Quint, hop inside. Let's talk."

"But, you're dead."

"No. But you will be if you don't get in here."

He flashed a laser gun. I looked around but there was no way out of this. I got into the van with him. The door slammed shut and the van pulled off. The front section was sealed off and I couldn't see who was driving. Kett pushed a button and the windows went opaque. He kept the laser gun pointed at me.

"So Quint, you've been busy."

"What makes you say that?"

"Working on the virus, meeting new people. I'm sure it's all very exciting. But it's also very stupid. You should have joined us when you had the chance."

"I take it the offer is rescinded. Too bad, I always wanted to work with a dead guy. So how is it you're alive and not lying at the bottom of a landfill?"

"That will all be explained soon enough. As for the offer, I wouldn't say it's rescinded. Anyway, my job is just to deliver you to the person who will explain everything."

"Ok, well I take that as a good sign."

"How so."

"If you were going to kill me, you wouldn't bother explaining things to me first."

"Well-reasoned."

"Thanks pal. Coming from a dead guy, that really means something."

We rode on in silence. Soon I could hear a garage door opening. We drove a little farther, then stopped. The van door opened and Kett led me through the garage to an elevator. Inside he waved a chip card with the crescent and wave symbol on it over the panel. We descended rapidly and as usual, my ears popped. When the elevator door opened we walked down a long corridor at the end of which was a security door. Again, he waved the chip, then pressed his fingertips against a small black panel. The thick metal door slid open slowly. Kett and I walked down past several doors until we reached the end of the hall and yet another security door. Another chip swipe and finger press and we were in a large room with a desk, chairs, and not much else. Very utilitarian, not very cozy. Kett gestured to one of the chairs.

"Have a seat. He'll be here in a minute."

"Who?"

"What, spoil the surprise?"

Kett left and the door slid shut behind him. I got up and searched the desk but it was empty. I walked around the room looking for a way out, but there was none. It was like the inside of a vault. I sat back down and waited. Searching through my pockets, I had nothing I could communicate to Heather and Max with. It was odd that Kett hadn't searched me for a com chip, even though I normally didn't carry one. How would he know that. Perhaps the room is insulated against radio transmission.

The door opened and Kett walked in, this time accompanied by the person I most expected to see.

"Joth. I see you've been working both sides of this equation."

"It's not much of an equation. Marea is beating Plexol, hands down, and we've only just begun. You don't look too surprised to see me, Quint. Was it that obvious?"

"It was getting more so all the time."

"I imagine you have a lot of questions for me, but I'm only willing to share so much at this point. Once you join us, of course I can tell you more."

"And what makes you so sure I'll join you."

"I have to admit that I was not being sensitive to your concerns before. Now that I better understand what you want, and since it's something I've got, I feel I can provide the proper motivation."

"Can you be a little less cryptic?"

"Of course. I have people working on resolving the memory loss issue. This digital dementia is of no use to me and will in fact hinder my objectives. We have beta tested several solutions, but none have shown much promise. Now obviously this has been one of many priorities on this project, and I only have 10% of my work force assigned to it. If you should decide to join us, I would be willing to increase that, thus increasing the odds that the anomaly is corrected."

"And I would be able to verify this how?"

"Oh, I suppose I could give you access to that database you've been trying to crack open. It has the time logs. The identity of my workers is of course encoded, so all you'll know for sure is which project a given worker is on and how many hours they spend per day on it."

"You could fake that."

"I suppose I could, but I won't."

"Lovely. And what exactly is it you want me to do?"

"More or less what I had you doing until you started messing things up for me. But that's partially my fault. I should never have agreed to let you back in at Plexol. It made sense at first, but I quickly realized it was a mistake."

"I don't understand, I thought what I was doing is trying to find you. Or at least, the person who turned out to be you."

"That's what you thought you were doing, and it's more or less correct. Really it was essentially penetration testing. I wanted to see how long it would take you, or anyone else who bothered to pursue the matter, to figure out who was behind the virus. You were doing a good job."

"Then why did you tell me I was messing up?"

"I needed an excuse to fire you, which I needed to do to get you out of the Plexol building before you did any more damage. My hope was you would drift off back to your dumpster. But instead you hooked up with Max and Heather. Which made you dangerous. And so, now I'm inviting you back to work for me, although now I'm switching you to penetration testing the virus re-installation program. I want to make sure there's no way for anyone to interfere. So you try to interfere, and from that we learn. Just as I learned several vulnerabilities in my plan and organization from your earlier work."

"And if I tell you to go get your circuit bent?"

"I guess my options are to lock you up somewhere or kill you. Each has its advantages. I'd have to think that over more. I kind of figured you'd agree."

"Why would I?"

"Quint, why the hell wouldn't you? Number 1, you hate Plexol. Here's an opportunity to help build the company that ultimately will crush them."

"Great, and then I can hate that company."

"You can help to shape it. What you've seen is only a tiny piece of the picture. My ultimate plan will be of massive benefit to mankind."

"By creating an army of shopping zombies with memory loss?"

"Quint, this project is still very much in beta testing. This isn't about shopping, it's about ultimately directing the course of history."

"And how do you get from here to there?"

"We can discuss that more later. Right now I need an answer from you."

"It's kind of relevant to what answer I give."

Joth sighed and got up from the desk. "Let's go on a tour of the facilities. I can explain more as we go along."

I got up and followed him out of the room, with Kett a few paces behind. We entered another room filled with servers. Joth gestured around. "This is the main computing room."

"These are Plexol servers."

"They were. I took them off the network and re-assigned them to my project."

"Wait, we're at Plexol?"

"Yes. In the sub sub sub basement. Or is it sub sub sub sub?"

"So you just pop down here, check on how the virus is going, then pop back up and continue your work for Plexol. Convenient. I guess you basically are a virus, living off the host corporation."

"That's good Quint, I hadn't thought of that. I like to think of it more as the tide washing out to sea, taking all the detritus out with it, then washing back in with fresh clean water."

"I take it you haven't spent much time at beaches. In my experience tides wash in more crap then they wash out."

Joth glared at me, then led me into the next room. There were monitors on the wall with maps, each with small colored dots. "These give us real time data for the location of the brain chip recipients."

"The chip has GPS?"

"No, unfortunately. That would be far more accurate. We use triangulation based on which g-wave towers are receiving the most recent transmissions from the chip. It's good enough for our purposes."

"You can tell if they went to the place you told them to go."

"Correct."

"How do you know if they made the purchase you directed."

"That's the easy part. Most stores use software designed by Plexol. We send them to one of those stores. Hacking into their sales database is a simple matter. But many of them are large chains and the data we have access to is aggregated across locations, so we use the chip's location to double check that the command was properly followed."

"You don't leave anything to chance."

"I can't. When we scale this up we'll need to know where our people are and whether they have followed instructions."

"And so what exactly will you be programming them to do?"

"You're familiar with the D-Plex touch screen, I assume."

"Of course, it's a little old tech, but I've seen a few still in use."

"Do you remember where?"

"Voting machines."

Joth smiled broadly, and as my words hung in the air, I realized why. He took me into the next room where there were about 20 voting machines with D-Plex touch screens. "These machines were 'borrowed' from randomly chosen locations throughout the country. We removed the main switch chips from each and examined them. You see, I had noticed a statistical anomaly, and I had a theory about what was causing it."

"If you're talking about the Heisen theory, that was debunked years ago."

"That's what most people think. I reviewed the voting data that Heisen based his theory on. It was startling. In almost every election where there was a candidate who ended up supporting legislation favorable to Plexol's interests, that candidate had won be an exceedingly small margin in a race that polls had predicted would go the other way."

"Yes, but I thought they examined the voting machines and determined there had been no fraud."

"Quint, I'm surprised at you. Who do you think examined the machines?"

"I would assume some government agency."

"They don't have anyone qualified for that. They had to outsource it. And guess who the lowest bidder was?"

"Please tell me it wasn't Plexol."

"Well, they were good enough to create a small corporation named Vo-tech, just to allay suspicion. But yes, it was all done by Plexol programmers, all of whom have subsequently risen through the ranks. Actually, I was one of them."

"So Plexol has been successfully manipulating elections all this time?"

"Yes. But I'm going to put a stop to that."

"It sounds like you're not so much putting a stop to it as taking it over."

"Fair enough. But I won't use that power just to create more power. I'll use it to benefit people. There is so much that could be done, we have so much technology and yet still there are poor people. It's a pathetic failure of mankind. Of our leadership"

"So instead of manipulating the voting machines, you're going to manipulate the voters."

"Both, actually, hitting the problem from two angles. We're working on a virus for the D-Plex, but there's time for that. We need to fix the problems with the brain chip program, then go back to implanting them on a mass scale."

"And what do you do about those pesky people who don't

want a brain chip?"

"Kill them with kindness. Thanks to the new revenue stream that will result from our 100% compliance advertising, we'll have every company on the planet begging to advertise with us. We can use that revenue to cut the cost of the brain chip so anyone can afford it. I suppose if there are still significant numbers who don't get the chip we can enact legislation requiring it. But I don't think it will come to that. Who wouldn't want 24 hour a day access to the cyberverse?"

"I guess someone that doesn't want to lose his memory."

"Quint, we are working on that. It's a glitch but we will fix it. And by joining us, you will be helping to shift resources to the resolution of that issue."

"Ok, so everything makes sense except for one thing. Why me? You don't really need me to do any of this. You could find someone else to do the penetration testing."

"All true, but you see I can't keep raiding Plexol for programmers. I've already poached too many and projects are falling behind. That's why I shifted the people in the cube farm upstairs back to their projects and off the virus. The lag time was getting too large. What I need are non-Plexol programmers, good ones. That's a pretty small group. Your experience is very valuable to me Quint."

"Well, I suppose I should be flattered. I'll be honest with you Joth, I don't buy all this feed the poor crap. I just don't see you as the type who really gives a crap."

"So you think I'm just after the power?"

"Frankly, yes."

"Fair enough. I suppose you'll have to wait and see whether I live up to my aspirations. But the brain chip virus is a reality, Quint. You can help shape that reality, or stand on the sidelines and watch it all happen. You can be the man to make sure this new power is used for ultimate good, or you can pat yourself on the back for staying pure. I would point out, not all the work you did all those years for Plexol has been used for good."

"Right, and I left. I rejected that."

"And what has that changed? Plexol is still there. At this rate, it will always be there. They have no pretensions to feeding the poor, curing society's ills. They are there to make money. Nothing more. To grow and grow and grow until they dominate the entire planet."

"They're pretty close to that already."

"Precisely why we must act now to bring them down and build something new in its place."

"Joth, if you really cared about people you would not be sticking a mind control chip in their brains and whispering commands to them, let alone creating the memory problems. You would be empowering people, not further enslaving them."

"They are already slaves to Plexol. I will set them free."

"By further enslaving them?"

"By collectivizing their power and using it for their common good."

"And you're in a better position than they are to decide what that good is?"

"I'm in a better position to see it through to fruition. Alone, they are powerless. United they have massive power. The possibilities once we harness that collective power are mind boggling."

He looked insane. He sounded insane. And so, I concluded, he probably was insane. There was no question of actually joining his effort, but it seemed like the best way to prevent him from succeeding would be to pretend to join and then sabotage from within. It was essentially what he was doing to Plexol.

Joth walked to one of the monitors and gestured toward the dots on the map. "One day there will be so many dots on the map, you won't see the map anymore."

"I'll join you but under one condition."

"What's that?"

"I want 100% resources devoted to the memory loss problem until it is solved."

"You know I can't do that. We have to keep the virus installed to continue our progress, and that takes a team devoted solely to fighting Plexol's countermeasures."

"You said yourself you've taken Plexol's people off that project and put them back on their old projects."

"There are still a few, plus there's an automated system in place that at random intervals re-installs the OS. And then there are people like your new friends, Heather and Max. No, I have to keep the virus up and running or the whole thing collapses, and that takes people devoted to keeping it running. I can put 20% on memory loss."

"90."

"Quint, you're worth a lot to me, but not that much. The only way I could devote more than 20% is if you helped recruit in more programmers."

I thought about this. If I could install a team of my own, we could collectively subvert Joth's plans. The more of his people I replaced with my own, the better.

"I might be willing to do that."

"Bonus points if you recruit the twins."

"Not likely. You know, their mother suffered memory loss from the chip. I don't suppose you have someone working on reversing the damage."

"Dr. Weinberg has been attempting to do that."

"He's one person."

"He's the best we've got. He has residents and researchers at his disposal. He's the head of a large department and he has Plexol's full backing."

"And so far no progress at all."

"The brain is a tricky thing, Quint."

"Thanks, I'll try to remember that. How many points do I get for each body I bring in?"

"I hadn't thought of it being so mechanical, but ok. I'll devote an additional 1% of total resources for each person you bring in."

"Make it 2%."

"You certainly enjoy negotiating."

"It's only fair."

"Ok. Done. I could use the additional brain power."

"So what's the arrangement, what's my pitch?"

"They get paid slightly more than a Plexol programmer, plus they get to work from home. They can have whatever gear they need to get their job done."

"Ok. I guess I better get started then."

"That's fine. I'll have Kett take you wherever you need to go."

"I see, and he'll make sure I don't stray off the path."

"Obviously, I do need to keep an eye on you, Quint. For now, anyway."

"Well, I'm ready to get going now."

"Kett, take Mr. Heldin where he needs to go to recruit new programmers. If there's any problem, let me know."

Kett nodded, then led me to the door. Joth called out, "Quint, don't double cross me. It won't go well for you."

"Wouldn't dream of it, Joth. If there's one thing I hate it's a double crosser."

Kett drove me to the address I gave him. We went up to the apartment together and paid a visit to Heather's friend Milos. He seemed surprised to see me, and even more so to see Kett. I walked in and gestured to Kett.

"Hi Milos, you know Kett I assume."

"Um, I don't recall . . . meeting him."

"Sure you do. I'm sure Joth introduced you two at some point, didn't he Kett?"

Kett stood silently, glaring at me. I glared right back.

"Come on, cut the crap boys. If we're all going to be working together we need to be friends."

Kett grabbed my arm. "Come on, let's get out of here, you can't recruit him."

"Why, because he's already recruited?"

Kett didn't say anything, just pulled me out the door. That was all the confirmation I needed. We got back in the van and Kett turned to me. "Where to now?"

"The Holo-News 10 building on Wozniak Way."

"I don't think so."

"I have a programmer friend there who might be interested in this project."

"How dumb do you think we are? We know you were on your way there before to expose the memory loss issue. That's why we picked you up."

"Ok, well that confirms another hunch I had. So you guys are bugging the twins' apartments."

He was quiet, and once more his silence spoke volumes. I thought through the implications. Surely, once Heather and Max realized I wasn't returning, they would go to the press themselves. Why hadn't Kett picked them up as well? There was only one way to find out.

"Ok, let's go to Plexol. I want to talk to Max and see if I can recruit him."

"No."

"Joth seemed pretty interested in that happening."

"If you're serious about recruiting Max you'll have to wait until he gets back from vacation."

"What vacation?"

Kett was thinking, and the effort caused small beads of sweat to break out on his forehead. "Look, let's go back to the lab. You need to get some work done and I need to talk to Joth before we make any more house calls."

We rode back in silence. This time I saw the entrance to the underground garage. We took the elevator down and Kett led me to a small computer lab with about 10 work stations. I sat down at one and explored the options. It was basically the same access I'd had when I was up in the cube farm. I noticed that there was no access to communication software, thus preventing me from contacting anyone. Well, that was the intent anyway. I had a few ideas on how to circumvent that limitation. But first I got up and checked out the room. The door was solid and locked. The vents were small, too small for a man to fit through. Joth was being careful, but I knew from experience that there were details he missed from time to time, and I was determined to find them.

Back at the workstation I searched for the encrypted database. As Joth had promised, I now had access to it. I could see an ID code that represented each worker. The next column showed a project code and the next showed hours spent that day on the project. There were additional columns of data, representing login and logout times, hours spent that week and month. A key explained the project codes. The only one that interested me was 80, the memory loss project. I could see that Joth had already begun reassigning people to the project. It was altogether possible this was a fake database created to keep me pacified. I tried to think of ways I could either prove or disprove the validity of the data I was looking at. It struck me that it was a Black Swan problem. Just as you can only prove that not all swans are white by finding a black swan, I could only prove that the database was fake by finding indications of data fabrication. I could not prove it was accurate. And so I thought through the ways to prove it was fake.

At the top of the monitor I saw that I was logged in as user 1138. I cross referenced this against the time log and found myself on there. It showed the correct time for when I had started working on this work station. But that didn't make sense, I hadn't logged in, I'd sat down randomly at a station and had instant access. On top of which I was not working on any project yet, but it was logging my time on the penetration test project. So either Joth was incredibly bad at logging time, or this was a fake.

I closed the time log and shifted focus to my next priority, finding Heather and Max and communicating with them. It was possible they were at work about 10 floors above me. Or Joth could have them locked up somewhere. There was an additional possibility that I didn't want to contemplate. They could be dead.

This led me to another thought. How on earth was Joth going to contain the information that the Plexol chip was causing memory loss. Surely there were enough people walking around with this knowledge that he couldn't bug and monitor them all. He couldn't kidnap them all as they were on their way to talk to the media. It was a non-trivial problem. Yet it was obviously a priority for him. He had picked me up to prevent me from going to the media. How was he managing the other people walking around who had a family member with brain chip related memory loss. And surely there had to be a number of Plexol programmers who, like Heather and Max, had connected the dots. How would he control all those people?

A sense of dread filled me, starting as a tightness around my chest and spreading quickly to every atom of my body. Had he somehow gotten brain chips into enough people that he had sufficient control to prevent a media report? He'd previously told me they were no longer installing the chip. Was this true? And he had mentioned a future price drop to increase the number of people with the chip. Had that already happened? Was there already an army of brain chip zombies walking around out there, preventing the information leak he feared? If so, then all these people were likewise going to suffer memory loss, were slowly suffering it already.

I once more shifted my focus to the task of finding the twins. If they were still out there somewhere, they could get the news out. They could stop this. It was our best chance. I logged in to the

normal time log for the cube farm workers to see if either Heather
or Max were logged in, but like the encrypted one, the users were
identified only by a number. There was no way to know who was
who. I stared at the data. Then it struck me. I knew what time Max
had been at work yesterday, around what time he'd left, and around
what time he had logged back in from his apartment. I ran a
Boolean search with these parameters and came up with 3 possible
users. Of those 3, only 2 were currently logged in. That wasn't a
good sign. I looked at the time log for the 3rd user and saw that it
most closely matched my recollection for the time Max logged
back in from Heather's apartment.

If Joth had Heather and Max picked up, surely he would have
made the same pitch to them as he made to me. After all, they
were both valuable programmers and he could use their skills.
Assuming they had agreed in hopes of sabotaging the system, they
would be logged in somewhere. The most likely project to have
them work on would be memory loss, since they had an incentive
to find a solution to that problem. So I needed to find them in the
system, and send them some type of message. Or plant a message
where they were sure to find it.

In order to solve the memory problem, they would have to
work on the code that controlled the memory wipe function. I
pulled up a copy of the virus source code on my monitor and
searched through until I found that section. I added a comment
line that read "Plx2GIGO2apt2Plx-Q". To any other coder
working on the project it would be meaningless, but Heather

would understand the meaning as the path I'd taken, from Plexol to GIGO to her apartment and back to Plexol again. She would know I was here. Max could probably figure it out too.

I saved the revised source code as the "current beta candidate v0.0," which didn't even make sense but would catch their eye and hopefully pique their interest enough to open it and look around. I then looked for new avenues of attack on the virus, since Joth had me working on penetration testing. Since I was already in the system, it didn't make much sense for me to launch a pen test. Why on earth had he given me full access? Was he testing me, watching to see what I would do? Or had he just given me standard login rights without thinking about it. I opened a new session without logging out of the old one, and in that session logged out of the system so I could approach it as an outsider. Then I tried to log back in. I used my employee ID as both username and password. It let me in.

This had to be a fake system. The whole thing. It made absolutely no sense at all. Joth was just toying with me, letting me play in my own little sandbox while he continued on with his plan. He could watch me find vulnerabilities in this fake sandboxed system, then apply what he learned to the actual system, without me ever having access to it. But there was a potential flaw in this approach. The console had to be running off the same servers as his real system. All I needed to do was find a way out of the sandbox and into the real system. I opened another session, then another session within that one, and continued on. At some point I was bound to reach the limits of my system. That would create an error and hopefully drop me out of the sandbox and into the real system.

Manually opening sessions within session was getting old fast. I opened a compiler, quickly hashed together some code to automate the process, and let it rip. There was a blur of windows opening within windows faster than the my brain could follow. After a few minutes the result I'd been after was before me. My home away from home. "Syntax Error." I hit return and there was a flashing cursor. I typed, "login" and was presented with a standard Plexol login screen. I tried my login from when I'd been working in the cube farm but they'd already removed it from the system. Then I remembered a quirk of the Plexol system. If you logged in from outside the building, you were only given 3 attempts to get the password correct. But if you were inside the building and wired into the network you had limitless login attempts. Joth had his own set of servers, but they were likely running the exact same OS as the main Plexol servers. In fact, they had to be connected to them somehow, because he had people switching back and forth between working legit and working for Marea, and needed a way to track them across both systems.

Back to the compiler. I put together a quick password cracker that would try random combinations of letters and numbers. I already knew the max characters for a Plexol system password was 100. I also knew that they wouldn't have deleted my login, just changed the password so they could retain any useful data from my sessions. It was out there somewhere, I just needed to hit the right password to get in.

I compiled the new program, and let it rip. It was trying approximately 1,000 different passwords per second. I sat back and waited, which got old fast. I moved to yet another console and logged in to the sandbox, poking around and seeing what else was in there. It occurred to me that perhaps Joth had kept his Plexol workers stuck in the sandbox when they were working on the virus. The messages we had decoded then would have been fakes. There was no real way of knowing what messages he was broadcasting to the brain chip.

I ran my sandbox buster on this console too, but once I was at the login I looked for ways to circumvent it. This went nowhere. I tried to restart the sandbox but couldn't view the directory structure or any file names. I moved to a new console, logged into the sandbox, and opened a cyberverse e-drop link. I didn't dare log into my actual e-drop, since there was likely a keyboard sniffer running, or the entire session was being logged. But I had several extra drops I used for frivolous things. Bits of code I wanted to save. Nothing essential. I logged into one of these. It worked, I was connected. I could see the files I'd loaded. This meant the sandbox was interacting with the real system and echoing back information. I attempted to open a com session so I could send a message directly to a random Plexol user. I typed in a user ID off the time log and wrote, "what's your progress on that project." I figured that was sufficiently vague that it wouldn't arouse suspicion.

An answer came back, "it's going well." I realized this could just be an artificial intelligence program. I needed to devise my own Turing test to be sure.

I typed, "I hear it's raining cats and dogs today."

The answer came back, "it's not raining at all."

"Not even a few cats?"

"Cats do not like water."

That was fast. It was likely AI, and didn't understand the expression, or my joking extension of it. Then again, some programmers can be pretty literal. I tried again to confirm my suspicion:

"What about catfish?"

"A catfish is a fish, not a cat."

"If a cat eats a catfish, is it a cannibal?"

"No, because a cat is not a fish, and a fish is not a cat."

Again, this sounded pretty computer-like. Also, why would a real person still be responding to this nonsense when they have work to do. I was going to take one more crack at it, more to amuse myself than anything else, when the password program beeped, indicating it had succeeded. I shifted back to the first console and looked at the open Plexol session. I was in. I pulled up a list of available users. Heather and Max were shown as being logged in, but not into the main system. I followed the trail and ended up at the encrypted database. This meant they were somewhere in the building, and likely somewhere down near my little dungeon. I needed to get out of this room and find them.

I got up and looked around. There was the ubiquitous

Plexol ceiling cam. I pulled a chair over, stood on it, and reached up. The tiny dome over it was made of a hard clear material. I thought about trying to crack it, but instead pushed up the ceiling tile next to it. It was hard wired. I yanked hard on one of the wires until it came loose. I got down off the chair and stood by the door, waiting. It opened and Kett walked in. I tripped him and pushed him to the ground, then grabbed the key chip out of his hand. I jumped up and left the room, closing the door behind me. I was back in the corridor and there were about 10 doors. I tried the closest one. It was the server room. I wouldn't have minded making a little mischief in there, but it would have to wait.

The next room was an empty office space. The door opened onto yet another corridor. This one had no doors and was curved so I couldn't see where it ended. I put that on my mental checklist of places to explore. I opened the next door and was happy to see Heather sitting at a computer. She turned to see me, jumped up and ran over, nearly knocking me over with a hug.

"Quint, where have you been, are you ok?"

"I'm fine, kid. How about you and your brother?"

"We're fine, he's in one of these computer labs."

"I've got the key, let's find him, then find a way out of here."

Two more doors opened to empty office space. The next one opened and there was Max. Heather ran over and hugged him while I checked the remaining doors. So far the curved corridor was the most promising. I lead the twins back there and we ran along the hallway which arced in a quarter circle, ending at a door.

126

I tried the key chip but it wouldn't open.

"There must be a different chip to open this one," I said.

"Let me try something," Max said. He pulled a p-rom chip from his pocket and attached it to the key chip. He started punching numbers into the small keypad and the small screen lit up. He held the key close to the door and continued manipulating the numbers. Suddenly there was a click and the door opened. Max smiled. "Plexol has a bad habit of incrementing lock codes based on a simple algorithm, it limits the number of possibilities."

"Well done," I said.

We walked through the door into a garage. There was an elevator door next to us. I pressed the button and we waited. It opened and we walked in. It was a standard Plexol elevator. We rode up to the main floor and got out on what I recognized as the back side of the building. There were emergency exits on this side, and leaving through one would set off an alarm. I turned to Heather and Max.

"We can go this way and run for it, or try to blend in with the crowd and go out through the lobby. Any thoughts?"

Heather looked around. "There aren't any guards nearby, we could probably get to the NanoRail before they catch up with us."

"And if the NanoRail doesn't show up for a while?"

"Then . . . that would suck."

Max looked up at the ceiling. "There are cameras all over the place. We need to do something now. Let's go for it."

I looked at Heather and she nodded. Just then I saw a

guard heading our way. I lunged for the emergency exit and the twins were close behind me. The guard started running. We ran to the NanoRail station. I could see a train pulling up as we neared the platform. People were boarding and the doors were about to close. I yelled out "wait!" and one of the passengers grabbed the door trying to keep it from closing. All three of us ran onto the train and the doors shut. The guard who was just steps behind us pounded on the door, but the train pulled out of the station. I saw him pull out a com chip and start talking into it. Max turned to me.

"Ok, now what?"

"I have a long list of places we can't go. And I have a list of criteria for wherever we do go, but I don't have any place in mind."

"Well, we can stay on here until we figure it out. We should probably switch lines every so often to be on the safe side."

"Good idea."

We looked around, found an area without any people and huddled together there. I filled them in on what had happened since I'd left the apartment. Then it was Heather's turn to fill me in.

"You were gone maybe an hour when I got a message from Milos for us to meet him at his apartment. We left our building and there was a van waiting for us. They took us here and we met with Joth. He gave us the same ultimatum he gave you. We pretended we would work for him, but of course we were just looking for holes in the system, something that would either help us to stop him, stop the virus, or get us out of there. Then you showed up. Oh Quint, I'm so glad to see you again"

"Same here."

"So what should we do?"

"I think our best bet is to contact the media. My buddy at Holo-News would be the obvious choice, except I think Joth had your apartment bugged, so now he knows about him. It would be the most logical place to wait for us. I guess we just need to go somewhere we've never mentioned, somewhere we don't know anyone."

"Well, if we can't go to Holo-News 10, let's go to Holo-News 12."

"Great. Any idea where they're located?"

Max pulled a utili-chip from his pocket and spoke into it. "Address, Holo-News 12." The screen showed us a map and the address. Max pointed. "We're over here, heading the wrong way. To get there we'll either have to go past Plexol again, or take this long route around town."

I looked at the map. "It will take us too long that way. Let's get off here and catch the next train inbound. We'll just have to take our chances."

Soon we were on a NanoRail heading back towards Plexol. The train filled up and by the time we got to the Plexol station the car was packed. I kept a sharp eye out for Plexol guards, but didn't see any around. We left the station and headed out towards our destination. 5 stations later we were there. We walked a block to a building with a large sculpture of a satellite out front. Inside we approached the front desk and I spoke to the receptionist.

"We need to meet with one of your reporters."

"Which one?"

"An investigative reporter."

Heather whispered in my ear, "Maybe whoever covers Plexol for them."

I whispered back, "No, they probably have him on the payroll." I turned back to the receptionist. "We have a great story. Big news. A scoop."

She gave a smile that said, I hear that every day. "Why don't you have a seat over there and I'll see who's available."

We sat down and huddled again. Heather looked concerned. "I don't think this is going to get us anywhere."

"You may be right. Hard to say, but I don't know what else to do."

"I do," Max said. He was looking off at a sign. It said, "Studio Tour." Max leaned toward me. "We'll stay put, you go on the tour. Find some way to get the message out."

He didn't have to tell me twice. I got up and went over to the bank of elevators near the sign. One was open. There was a uniformed man standing near it. He smiled. "Next tour is in half an hour."

"Oh," I said, "Gee that's too bad. I left my key chip on a table up there, I just need to go back up and get it."

"I'll have to get someone to escort you, wait here."

He walked off and as soon as he was around the corner I hopped on the elevator and hit a button that said "Studio." When it opened I walked down a hall and saw what was obviously a mockup of a studio. This was no good. I walked up and down the hallway but found nothing else of interest, other than the stairs. I took them down a floor and came out into another hallway. I could see the lights of a real studio and there was the anchor man surrounded by the holo-cams. I tried the studio door but it was locked. I tapped on the glass and one of the technicians saw me and came to the door. He pointed up to a sign that said "On The Air." I pulled a chip card out of my pocket and gestured to it as though it was something he might need. He looked confused but took the bait and opened the door. I nearly knocked him over running in and over to the anchor, who stopped mid-sentence, looked at me and said, "who the hell are you?"

"Quint. I used to work at Plexol. The Plexol brain chip has a virus that causes memory loss. They've been aware of the problem for some time but have refused to alert the public or do a recall." The anchor gestured to one of the technicians who hit a button. I could see on the monitor that they'd gone to a commercial. The tech picked up a com chip and whispered into it while the anchor backed away from me. Soon I saw a uniformed man running to the studio. I looked for an escape but there was only one door. I walked calmly to the door and waited for him. He came in, grabbed me by the arm, and escorted me to the elevator and back to the lobby. Heather and Max were standing pointing at a large monitor.

"We saw you. It was amazing."

"Glad you liked it."

The guard shoved me out the door and Heather and Max came running after me. Heather threw her arms around my head and gave me a sloppy kiss. "I'm so happy right now. We should have done this long ago."

I discretely wiped some Heather slobber off my face and gave her a peck on the cheek. "Well, it remains to be seen what reaction this gets. People might think I'm just some crank, or dismiss the whole thing as a hoax. At minimum though, it's got to have the Plexol brass squirming."

"So now what?"

"We need a safe place to hole up and get to work on removing the virus."

Max said, "we had a whole team at Plexol working on that damned virus and got nowhere."

"That's because Joth was dumping you into a sandbox. You were never working on the actual virus, just a virtual virus. He had everything walled off just to be on the safe side. But we can get around that and work on the real deal. When we were stuck in the room I found a new password to my old Plexol account. We can use that to get back into the main server, then worm our way back to Joth's secret servers and attack the virus directly."

Heather thought this over. "If we remove it Joth will notice."

"True."

"But if we replace it with a harmless version . . ."

"Exactly what I was thinking. My god, beauty and brains all in one package."

She smiled and squeezed my arm. Max pulled the utili-chip from his pocket. "I have a friend with a decent set up and he doesn't work for Plexol. He's a programmer for United Robotics. Let's swing by his place."

It was a quick trip there. We were greeted at the door by Max's friend, a tall skinny guy with long straight hair that looked like it had last been washed during the space age. He stuck out a skinny hand to shake.

"Nacho."

"Nacho?"

"Yeah. That's what everyone calls me."

"I'm Quint, glad to meet you."

He showed us his place. There were bits of gear all over the place, some of it moving under its own power, including a robotic arm that was crawling along the floor like a snake.

"Make yourselves at home. There's fresh coffee in the kitchen."

That was music to my ears. I poured coffee for myself and the twins, then we sat down at Nacho's console. I let Max have the seat of honor. I gave him the username password combo and he logged in. He said over his shoulder, "how long until Joth realizes we're in the system?"

"Hopefully he's got bigger fish to fry with our recent

broadcast. It should buy us enough time to get in there and hack the virus."

Max worked his way down to Joth's server, then we hit the same wall of encryption as before. I stared at the monitor. "Damn, if only we had the laptop."

"Oh yeah, I forgot to tell you." Max pulled the laptop out of his shoulder bag. "We do."

He set it up and opened the program that had been working on a portion of the encrypted database. We had enough information now to do a targeted attack on the full database, which likely contained the source code for the real virus. Max was switching from program to program on the laptop, putting together algorithms. He copied this over to the console, then ran his attack. We simultaneously took sips of our coffee, watched and waited. Heather walked over to the holo-viewer and flipped it on to see if there was any discussion of our little announcement. Holo-News 10 was talking about some sporting event. Holo-News 12 however had a reporter saying they had contacted Plexol to confirm or deny our allegations. So far no response. I called over to her, "at least they're talking about it. The longer Plexol delays making an announcement, the bigger the story becomes and the more people will be talking about it."

Max called over his shoulder, "I'm in."

I walked over. He was already downloading the virus source code. He then copied it over to the laptop and handed it to me. "I'll work on the console, you take a crack at it on the laptop. Heather, you get on the com chip and contact every media outlet there is, telling them that you have independent proof of the Plexol virus which we would be happy to send them a copy of. I've put a copy on this chip for you."

We all got to work. It felt good to be working with these two. The virus code was nearly identical to what we'd seen in the sandbox version. I quickly located the memory wipe function and looked it over. I called over to Max, "I'm thinking we just delete this whole chunk in the memory wipe loop, comment out the whole thing."

"We need to leave in the confirm message, but otherwise I agree."

"I'll do it on this version, you look through the rest of the code and make sure there's nothing crucial we're missing."

Max laughed. "When hundreds of thousands of brain chip users become consciously aware of the messages they've been receiving, all hell will break lose."

Heather said, "but what about those who have already suffered memory loss. The messages could still be effective on them."

Max looked serious again. "I hadn't thought of that. Quint, you keep working on the memory wipe loop, I'm going to find the message and dreamvertising code and see what we can do."

We got back to work. I had the easy job and was quickly done. I split up the message code with Max and we both worked at that. It was intertwined with several subroutines, some of which were used by other parts of the code, so we couldn't just comment everything out. It was like performing surgery, cutting just what we needed to without damaging anything else.

Time flew by. Occasionally Nacho would come over to see what we were up to, then he'd drift off to tinker with his robots. I got up to stretch my brain and see what he was working on.

"You know, I considered United Robotics before I got sucked into the Plexol vortex. Decent place to work?"

"Look at it this way. I'm sitting around playing with toys and getting paid for it. They allow us each one day a week to just experiment, play around. It's actually resulted in some of the greatest R&D advances they've had."

"Sounds good. So what are you working on?"

"My specialty is self-sufficient robots and robots that can build robots. Right now I'm working on a robot that will go around looking for fixable flaws in my other robots, and fix them."

"Sounds like there would be a fair amount of artificial intelligence required for that."

"Less than you'd think. It works through a flow chart. Of the flaws I've noted in past work, my own and that of my co-workers, about 80% can be categorized and added to the flow chart. Only the remaining 20% would be unique and require human intervention. By letting robots handle the 80%, it frees us up to do what we're best at."

"And I assume this is just the start of a larger project. I mean, the lesson here could be applied to any number of situations."

"Exactly. It's about dividing the world into those things that are best handled automatically, and those that are best handled by humans."

"That's fascinating stuff. Just do me a favor."

"What's that?"

"Hold off on replacing programmers with robots until I'm old enough to retire."

Nacho smiled. I wandered back to the laptop and went back to work on the code. Heather was still contacting various media outlets. Max was hacking through the code. I could see it was going to be a long night.

7.

By morning I'd taken about 3 or 4 cat naps. In between I'd managed to make substantial progress. Heather was curled up asleep on the couch, having run out of places to contact. Max was in the midst of a nap, and I got up to look at his console and see where he was in the process. He had fallen asleep with his face on the keyboard and there was an endless string of M's on the monitor. I nudged him awake and said, "why don't you go lay down, I can take over for a while."

He got up looked around, and laid down on the floor. I deleted the string of M's, then looked through the code he'd been working on. He had finished re-working the code for the most part and was debugging. I ran his code through some tests of my own. It seemed solid. Nacho came out of his room and let out a long, low yawn, then he came over to see what I was doing.

"Looks like you're debugging."

"It's Max's code, I'm just checking it over. It would be nice if we had a brain chip to test it on."

"Coming right up."

Nacho went rummaging through a closet, tossing bits of gear behind him as he dug deeper and deeper. Then he called out, "aha, here it is," and came out with a white cylinder with two black eyes and a smiley mouth painted on it. He set it down next to me.

"It's got a brain chip inside, surrounded by a model of the human brain. You can beta test your code on here and see what happens."

"Plexol has these but they look a little more . . . realistic."

"Typical. They waste time making it look pretty. Mine will work just as well as theirs."

I plugged a cord from the white cylinder into a jack on the console and fired up the code. I opened a second window to see the resulting readings and ran a few tests. Cyberverse access was fully functional. There was no dreamvertising, and no memory erasing. It worked. I ran a few more tests, then woke up Max to show him the results. He ran a few tests of his own and when he was satisfied with the results we compiled the code and uploaded it to the Plexol server. We hacked into the OS overwrite function, and broadcast the new version of the virus to every Plexol brain chip out there. I shook Max's hand.

"Great coding. There were some elegant solutions in there."

"Thanks. I liked what you did with the memory loss loop."

"That was the easy part. What you did was . . . art."

Heather woke up and looked at us bleary eyed.

"Is it done?"

"We just sent it out."

"And how do we know Joth isn't just going to replace it with the real virus."

Max said, "I added a notification system, similar to the one he had but with a few variations. It will automatically notify us if anyone tries to tamper with the code, then it will shut down all functioning. There won't be any way to write new code to it."

"Ok, so now what do we do."

"Sleep?"

I added, "sounds like a good idea."

Heather looked at us both like we were nuts. "Guys, we just pushed a boulder up a hill, now it's time to push it down the other side. We've stopped the virus from doing any more damage, we've done everything we can to get the media interested in this story. Now we have to expose Joth so he's held accountable for what he's done. And we need to get the medical community involved so they can work on undoing the brain damage that's been done to all these people."

Max said, "you know, those are all important things. But we could sleep a few hours and then do all that. Eating might be nice too."

I added, "there's something else to consider too. Joth still has control of the voting machines. We haven't even begun to tackle that angle. By exposing it, we not only expose him but Plexol. Of course, we also then expose a lot of powerful people who were put in office by Plexol. So that could get a little messy."

Heather thought this over. "One thing at a time. It's months until the next election. Hopefully then we'll have sufficiently damaged Plexol that opening an investigation into their voting machine fraud will be easier. For now we need to focus on the brain chip. We need to organize a call for accountability. Who at Plexol knew what when? Joth can't be the only one who knew about the memory loss, even if he is the only one behind the virus itself. They failed to recall a dangerous product or alert the public. I think that's the issue we push first."

Max asked, "so what's the first step?"

"The first step is keep the pressure on the media to investigate this story. I'm going to see who's picking up the story, then offer to set up interviews with Plexol programmers who worked on the virus. That being us. In the meantime, yes, get some sleep."

Max said, "you won't have to tell me that twice." and fell onto the couch. A few minutes later he was snoring. Heather was checking the holo-viewer to see who was covering the virus story. I sat down in a large overstuffed chair and took a quick cat nap. In part of my dream I saw Josie walking away from me. When I woke up I thought about her. I'd been avoiding thinking about her for too long. When I saw Kett alive, though, I realized something I'd been worried about. She had only pretended to kill him. She'd been in Joth's back pocket all along. For her, it was just another job. It didn't matter to her that she was playing me for a fool. When had that ever mattered to her.

I looked over at Heather. She was beautiful, smart, friendly.

Why didn't I feel as strongly about her as I did about Josie. What was it that Josie had. Was I just attracted to the sadness in her eyes, or was it more demented than that. Was it the crappy way she treated me. That was a depressing thought. Was I really that screwed up. Was there a way to become un-screwed up.

I got up and walked over to Heather. "So? Are they picking up the story?"

"Just barely. I feel like I've used up all my kindling and still don't have a fire. We may have underestimated the extent to which the press is controlled by Plexol. Most of the stories I've seen so far take the angle of 'crazy man breaks into Holo-News 12 studio.' The good thing is it gives them an excuse to show the footage of you, looking decidedly un-crazy. But no one has mentioned communication to them confirming what you said on the air. I think they're afraid to take this from a novelty story to a real story."

"Ok, well maybe the media isn't going to solve this problem for us. Maybe we need a new strategy."

"Like what?"

"Go directly to the masses. Tell them what's happening."

"How? Post information on the cyberverse? It will be seen as just more craziness in a sea full of the stuff."

"Why don't we go even more direct. Communicate to the brain chip users via their brain chip."

Heather thought this over. "You and Max removed the code that allows that type of communication."

"True, but we could add it back. Or just hard wire in the

message we want to deliver."

"That would require a re-install, which if I recall correctly you made impossible."

"Heather, I've been programming for decades, and never once have I completed a project without creating a back door."

"So we can do it?"

"Yes. Let's agree on the phrasing of the message and I'll make it happen."

We sat down and brain stormed, ultimately agreeing on the following, "Warning, the Plexol brain chip can cause memory loss. See your doctor about having it removed as soon as possible. Contact your elected official and ask what they are doing about Plexol's gross negligence." It wasn't exactly poetry, but it got the point across.

I sat at the console and added the message to the virus code. It would be delivered three times, then stop. Next, I beta tested the revised code on the white cylinder, and then logged back into the Plexol server to open the back door and send the code through. But there was a problem. The back door didn't work. I pinged the brain chip OS and received back a version number that was different from the one we had written. Somehow, a new version was running.

"Heather, wake up Max. We've got a problem."

Once Max was up I explained what I'd found. He sat at the console and ran the ping again. Same result. He looked at me.

"This is not good. Joth has completely circumvented our

efforts. He's running his version of the virus again."

I scratched my head. "I don't see how it's possible. We covered all the bases. We did some solid coding. We tested it all out."

"Is it possible he found your back door?"

"While I hate to think that's it, I don't see any other more logical conclusion."

"So then we need to find a way back into the chip and load an updated version that lacks the back door."

"But Joth as somehow blocked us out of the device. It's locked."

"Then we need to find a key."

Max logged into the Plexol system and found the new version of the virus, copying it to a chip. "We need to go back to square one, sort through the source code."

"Wait, that's it. He must have left a fake version of the source code. There's something in the actual code we don't know about that lets him control who can update the OS."

Max looked at the code, then back to me. "This isn't good. Joth has us running in circles. We've accomplished almost nothing other than losing sleep."

"Keeping us busy seems to be his overall strategy."

"But why?"

"More penetration testing. Every avenue we search down, he closes up. Eventually there will be no flaws in his plan."

Max stared at the console, then back at me. He looked devastated. "I can't believe we've gone from winning to losing again.

I can't believe that asshole is going to succeed. I can't believe that he's been able to use us as one more tool in achieving his goals. There has to be a way."

Heather suddenly called us both over. She was pointing at the holo-viewer. "Quint, isn't that your guy?"

On the viewer was Dr. Weinberg, being interviewed by Holo-News 10 anchor Chad Blakey. Weinberg was holding up a brain chip. "I've been removing these because of the memory loss they've been shown to cause. It seems only the Plexol brain chips have this problem."

Chad asked, "But doctor, I have a Plexol brain chip and I've suffered no memory loss."

"How long have you had it?"

"I just got it last month."

"It's too soon for you to have measurable memory loss, but even as we speak it is causing seemingly irreversible brain damage. I would highly recommend that you and everyone else out there with the chip have it removed as soon as possible. The results of not doing so will be devastating."

We looked at each other in shock. Finally, the media was taking the story seriously. Heather took Max's hand. "You see, we can do this. We just have to keep at it. We're making progress."

Max smiled back at his sister. "So all our programming amounted to nothing, and all your work has paid off. Nice job, Heather."

"I think it's time I contact my friend at Holo-News 10," I said.

Heather looked concerned. "Won't that be risky?"

"It is, but we need to keep this momentum going, and that's the quickest way to get someone to take us seriously. The media could lose interest in this in a second. We have to keep it front and center. I think it's worth the risk."

"We should go with you."

"Absolutely not. If Joth intercepts me, so be it. He's only got one of us. But you two will still be working on getting the message out. I'll carry a com chip and if there's any trouble I'll let you know."

"Contact us every 20 minutes in any event. That way, if we don't hear from you, we'll know you ran into trouble," Heather said.

"Will do."

"And don't just program it to send us an 'I'm ok' message every 20 minutes."

I gave her a hug that ended up lasting longer than I planned. She felt good in my arms. I kissed her goodbye and was on my way.

The News 10 building was oddly similar to the News 12 building. I had my friend Wes paged. He came off the elevator smiling and waving.

"Quint, you're a celebrity."

"Glad to know I've already got a fan club."

"I missed the live feed but I watched the vidcap about 15 times. Unbelievable. That's Quint. That's my Quint. Oh man. Great stuff. So are you going to be hijacking one of our studios today?"

"I was hoping to get invited in this time."

"I can arrange that. For sure. But I have to warn you. The angle they're going to take is, here's that crazy guy. They will be asking you about how you did it. I doubt they'll ask much about the Plexol virus."

"Just get me on the air. I've watched enough politicians on holo to know the old trick. Answer the question you wish they'd asked you."

"Ok, man. Let's go upstairs, I'll show you what I've been working on, then introduce you to the new producer I work with and see what we can set up."

"Thanks Wes. I knew you'd help me out."

"Quint, you're helping me out. We get bonuses for bringing in anything worth broadcasting. I'm likely to get 100 credits out of this."

"Good, then drinks are on you after we're done."

"That's a deal."

Wes took me up to the programming suite. It had a modern design and some truly impressive equipment. Every work station had a holographic display with touch and motion sensors. You could do your programming the old school way, pounding on a keyboard, or actually manipulate programming objects in 3D space, assembling the program like a child plays with blocks. Wes sat down and showed me some of his work.

"I've got my own library of programed blocks that I reuse over and over, then there's a shared library with more stuff in it. Say I need a spinning logo to fly in over the anchor's head, then explode like fireworks, then morph into stars in the night sky. I grab this, this and this, toss them together, type in a few variables, and boom."

In seconds he was able to finish and play what he had just described.

"It's as close to going directly from your mind to a finished program as you're going to get."

"Impressive stuff, Wes, but I hope you're not losing your programming chops playing around with blocks all day."

"Oh, not at all. I spend half my time programming new modules to add to the library. Always keeping things fresh. I also coordinate with the design department. They'll send a 3D sketch and I'll bring it to life. It's a good collaboration. I love working with creative people."

"So I guess I should have docked my ship here instead of Plexol."

"Quint, you went for the big bucks. Not that I'm judging. I thought long and hard about going that route. I still wonder if I'd be doing more significant work if I had worked for Plexol, instead of all this eye candy. But in the end I'm happy with what I'm doing."

"Yeah, well you made the right choice Wes. Maybe when I'm done being the latest 5 minute celebrity I can get a gig here."

"You know I'll do everything I can to help."

"Thanks Wes. You're the last of a dying breed."

"Come on, let's go talk to my producer, Chak."

Wes lead me down the hall to a large office with glass walls. Inside was a large man behind an old wooden desk. Hanging on the wall was a real antique, one of the last typewriters produced sometime around 2014.

"Chak, I want you to meet an old friend of mine, Quint."

Chak stood up to shake hands. He had a big meaty hand that swallowed mine whole. "Glad to meet you Quint. Wes mentioned that he knew you when we picked up the News 12 feed of your little . . . incident. Good stuff. Takes balls. Or you're crazy. Either way, I wouldn't mind putting together a quick segment with you."

"That's exactly what I'm here for. My hope is that you guys will dig into this Plexol story."

"Well, don't hold your breath. Plexol is our number 1 advertiser, and we try not to piss in the drinking pot. I can get away with a 'look at this nutty guy' type of story, but I'm doing an expose."

"So how do I get someone to take the story and run with it?"

"Quint, I've been in this business a long time, and the days of true investigative journalism are long gone. Media consolidation has created an environment where all we can do is happy news and human interest. We try to sneak in a little substance here and there, but mostly we're not different from any other entertainment outfit. We need to have so many viewers to sell ads for so many credits. Everything else is just icing. I wish I could tell you otherwise, but that's just how it is. Sure you might find some cyberverse rag run out of some guy's closet that would be interested in this type of stuff, but no one will ever find it or read it. To really get a story out there it needs Plexol's blessing."

"Well, I've got to give it a try."

"Ok. Sam Peters is just finishing his noon report. Let's sit down with him and set up the interview. The angle I'd like to take is he opens with a normal story, then you walk in as though you've broken into the studio. He'll have some scripted questions for you, then off you go."

"Whatever it takes."

"I like that attitude. And since you're a friend of Wes, I'll try not to make you look like too much of a buffoon."

"Much appreciated."

Wes went back to work and Chak took me to the studio. We waited for Sam to finish his report, then Chak took me in and introduced me. Sam was all smiles.

"This should be fun. I enjoyed your News 12 bit. Good entertainment. Drama. People love that stuff."

"Glad I could amuse. You know, this studio is almost identical to the one at News 12."

"We're owned by the same parent company, use the same design team."

"Wait, I thought 10 and 12 were rivals."

"Most people think that. We do a lot of marketing to push people to one or the other based on demographics. That allows us to deliver a more specific group of viewers to the advertisers. It results in higher ad rates."

"Amazing. You guys have it all down to a science."

"Well, the guys who didn't have it down to a science disappeared. We're what's left. I guess it's economic Darwinism."

We went through his interview questions and rehearsed my cue to enter the studio. Part of me detested creating this phony media event, but I knew it was the best way to get the message out.

Sam was about to go back on the air when my com chip buzzed. I checked and it was Heather. I buzzed her back to let her know I was fine, then texted, "turn on News 10." Sam started talking, and when he got to my cue I walked in and stood next to him.

"I'm Quint Heldin, a former Plexol employee, and I have an important message for you and everyone out there."

"Wait, aren't you the same guy that broke into another holo-studio this week?"

"Yes I am. I'm letting people know about the danger of using the Plexol brain chip, which causes memory loss."

"But, how did you get in here, past all our security?"

"The brain chip has a virus which Plexol knows about, but they have failed to warn people. If you have one of these chips implanted, get it removed immediately."

"Do you plan on breaking in to any other holo-studios?"

"I will if that's what it takes to get the word out that Plexol and its management must be held accountable for their gross negligence."

"Before my security guards take you away, can you tell us what it's like to be an instant celebrity?"

"It gives me the opportunity to warn people that one of the programming managers at Plexol, Joth Wilb, is the person who created this dangerous virus. He has his own set of servers underneath the Plexol building in a sub sub sub basement, and is sending messages out to the brain chips in an effort to control the behavior of those who have the chip."

"Well, that's all the time we have, thanks for stopping by. Next up, a cheese eating contest that will surprise you, and some upcoming discounts on the new gadgets and gear you crave."

The floor manager signalled we were off the air. Sam turned to me and shook hands. "Thanks for stopping by, Quint. Nice to meet you."

"Did anything I said make you want to know more? Did it sound like something that would get people riled up?"

"To be honest, I was paying attention to my delivery, I didn't actually listen to your answers. I need to focus on my performance."

"Hm, well you might want to look into this brain chip story. It's causing brain damage, and Plexol knows it, and they've done nothing to stop it."

"Well, I'm sure they know what they're doing. Nice to meet you."

I wandered out of the studio. Chak came down the hall with Wes. They were both smiling.

"Wes can see you out, Quint. I've got a desk load of work but just wanted to thank you for stopping by."

"Thanks for letting me on the air."

"I wish there were more I could do . . ."

"So do I."

Wes and I went down to the lobby. We made plans to get together for a drink in a week, and soon I was on my way back to the apartment.

8.

Heather ran to the door and gave me a big hug when I walked in.

"That was great. I can't believe you said all that stuff about Joth."

"Yeah, I kinda figured why not. Get everything out there. It kind of confuses things a little, but what the hell. I guess I was hoping maybe someone at Plexol would start an internal investigation, even if the press has no interest in pursuing the matter."

Max was hacking away on the console. I walked over to see what he was working on. It was the encrypted database. I shook my head.

"You know, that could just be another fake. You could crack that open and find nothing but fake data inside."

"I know, but what else can we do. He's outsmarted us."

"Well, that's because he's been making the rules. We need to take a fresh approach to this thing."

"I'm all ears."

"I've only gotten as far as 'fresh approach' so far."

"Well, let me know when you come up with something else. Meanwhile, I'm going to play with this. I find it relaxing."

I walked back to Heather and we sat down on a couch. As usual, she was pressed right up against me, but I was starting to get used to that. Starting to need it. She said, "what if we get one of the extracted brain chips and copy the virus from it, then decompile that. We might find a flaw in the code we can exploit."

I gave her a kiss on the forehead. "Baby, I love that brain of yours. Looks like I'm making another field trip."

I got up. Heather grabbed my hand. "Now where are you off to?"

"Dr. Weinberg. He's been doing extractions, he would have a brain chip with the current virus version running on it."

"But he can't possibly still be doing work for Plexol after he went public."

"True, but that was just today. He would still have the chips. All I need is one recent one."

"What if Joth grabbed him?"

"Well, I guess I could call over first, but I don't want to tip anyone off. Better if I just show up. I'll be back before you know it."

"I'm going with."

"No you're not. Stay here and keep that brain of yours working. You're our secret weapon."

Another hug and kiss and I was out the door.

The hospital was busy. Dr. Weinberg was in surgery so I waited in the lobby. After 30 or so minutes a nurse came to get me. Dr. Weinberg was sitting in his office surrounded by his stacks of papers. He got up to shake hands, then we both sat down. He had a big smile.

"I saw you on the 3D TV thing, and I thought, hey, I need to speak out too. I'm glad you did that."

"Well, I'm glad you spoke out too, since everyone seems to think I'm some kook."

"There's worse things you could be. So were those papers helpful to you?"

"They were. But we've been unable to eradicate the virus. Our hope is that you could give us a recently removed brain chip from which we could extract a copy of the virus, and then work on finding a way to stop it."

"I'd be happy to help. Wait right here."

He left the room for a minute, then came back with a paper bag. "I tossed a dozen or so chips in here, all from this week. I figure it's best to give you a few extras in case they were damaged during the extraction."

"This is perfect. Thanks so much."

"No, thank you. It takes guts to stand up to a huge entity like Plexol. At my age I really don't care, it's worth the risk. But you better be careful. They are not going to take this lightly."

"Very true."

I got up and we shook hands again, and then I went back to the apartment.

Heather and Max stared at the chips as I poured them out of the bag and onto the table. Max picked one up and looked at it closely. There were tiny, the size of a small bead. "How on earth do we extract the virus from this thing?"

"I was hoping you two would have some ideas. I suppose we can put it in the white cylinder and fire it up, then poke around until we find a way to download the virus."

Max called Nacho over and they opened up the tin head. Nacho grabbed a tool that looked like a long tweezers with a magnifier screen attached to it. He carefully extracted the brain chip from the cylinder and set it in a small case, which he stuck in his pocket. He then took one of the new chips and inserted it. He closed up the tin head and we hooked it up to the laptop. We sent several messages to the chip and recorded the resulting output. Heather was staring off into space, but suddenly said, "try a peek at a187e." We both turned to look at her.

"That's pretty specific Heather," Max said, "where's that coming from?"

"I'm looking over Weinberg's papers again. That should be where the first line of the OS is stored."

Max tried it and sure enough, the first line of the OS came spitting back at us. He swiftly created a script that would peek each subsequent number and string the results together. Within seconds he had downloaded the whole thing and had it up on the screen.

He ran it through the decompiler and started sorting out the code into meaningful chunks.

"I'm going to dump this onto the console so you can look it over. I'm not done sorting it out, but you probably have your own method of doing that anyway."

I sat down at the console and started working over the code, putting it in blocks and diagramming the relationship between them. I had a flowchart program open and was keeping track of what I was doing there. Little by little the code revealed itself. It was actually similar to the fake code we'd been given to work on before, which made the process a lot easier. But the differences were significant.

"Max, are you seeing the internal message loops?"

"Yup. Even if the chip for some reason can't receive external messaging, it still has a reserve of stock messages to communicate to the user, followed by the brain wave manipulation. Some of these are pretty creepy. It seems like it's setting up the user to be more susceptible to the other messages."

Heather read over his shoulder. "Accept authority. Obey the commands. Do not question. Good god, he's creating an army of sheep."

"It makes me wonder," I said, "do you think the memory loss is intentional? Maybe it's a feature, not a bug. Maybe it's part of the overall goal, controlling people on a massive scale. Not just to do things like buy a certain product or support a certain candidate. Maybe it goes even beyond that. Create a world where the masses comply with one leader's every command."

Max opened a new program on the laptop. "I'm going to keep recording any output from the device in case Joth sends any new messages. It would be interesting to see what he's sending out there. It might confirm what you're saying."

I continued diving into the code, getting lost in it until Max called out, "I'm getting a new message."

The three of us looked at his screen where the message was being transcribed in real time. It said, "I will find them, and when I find them, I will respond."

Heather grabbed my arm. "Find who?"

Max opened a second window that showed an image coming through the chip. 4 pictures, 1 of me, 1 each of the twins, and 1 of Dr. Weinberg. Heather's grip on my arm tightened. "He's using them as a spy network, as informants. He can track us just by keeping tabs on the responses he receives from the brain chip users. If they see us they let him know, and he knows where the user is located."

I turned to face her. "Heather, I think we better all stay put. It could be very dangerous for us to be seen out there."

We need to warn Dr. Weinberg," she said.

"How do we do that without leaving the apartment?"

Suddenly Nacho appeared from his room. "Hey guys, I'm going out to get some pizza. Anyone else hungry?"

We all smiled at each other. Heather pulled a credit chip from her pocket. "I think you better stock up on more than just pizza.

You fly, I'll buy."

"Sounds fair to me."

"And while you're out there, could you do us a favor and stop by the hospital? We need you to deliver a message to a friend of ours."

"The hospital?"

"On second thought, you better not go there. I'll give you my com chip. Once you're away from this building you can use it to contact Dr. Weinberg and warn him that There are people out looking for him."

"That's pretty ominous. Are you sure about this?"

"Yes."

Heather gave him the com and credits. Nacho tucked them away and left. Heather looked concerned. "You don't think I'm putting him in danger do you?"

Neither me nor Max answered. Heather started toward the door but I grabbed her. "You can't go out there. He'll be fine. Just stay here with us."

"But what if . . ."

"Look, they have no interest in him, we're the ones they are looking for. I'm sure he'll be fine."

"Really?"

"Yes."

"What if they track the location of my com chip?"

"By the time they get there they'll have no way of knowing who used it. In any event, they would be looking for you, not

Nacho."

"I hope you're right."

"Me too."

We sat down on the couch. I put my arm around Heather and pulled her close. Max got up and wandered off, calling over his shoulder, I'm going to grab a little sleep. Wake me up in a half hour if I'm not up by then. Or if there's a new message from the brain chip."

Heather buried her face in my neck. "Quint, it's all starting to catch up with me. For a while this all felt like a dream, but now it suddenly feels so real. Do we really know what we're doing? How on earth can we topple something this big?"

"I know. I feel like I'm riding waves where one moment I'm floating and the next I'm drowning, overwhelmed. But we have to keep trying. If we don't stop Joth now, we'll never be able to."

She sat in silence for a while, then looked up at me. "There's one thing that doesn't make sense. Why would Joth allow Dr. Weinberg to continue removing the chips? Doesn't he want to increase the number of people with them installed?"

"I imagine it was a way of placating Weinberg, making him think he was solving the problem so he wouldn't go public. Meanwhile, Joth probably has other doctors installing more brain chips in a day than Weinberg can remove in a month. Or maybe . . ."

"What?"

"Forget it, I'm just speculating."

"Tell me."

"Well, I'm just thinking, what if the brain chip creates some permanent change in the brain that leaves the user open to Joth's communications by some other medium. Maybe broadcast over the holo-viewer, or via a com chip. Latent commands he can call into action remotely without using the brain chip."

I could feel Heather shiver against me. "Quint. Can we really make a difference? Is there really any chance we can stop him?"

"You better hope so. You better believe so. Otherwise, all is lost."

We held each other for a long time.

9.

Nacho came back loaded down with groceries. He opened the bags and showed us everything he'd gotten. There was enough food to keep us happy and well fed for a long time. As we helped put the food away, he told us about his call to Dr. Weinberg.

"I called him up, finally got past the receptionist to the nurse and past the nurse to the doctor. He said he knew he was in danger but didn't care. But he was very nice, thanked me for calling. Nice guy."

Heather said, "I wish there were some way we could get him over here with us. He could help us work on an overall strategy for bringing an end to Joth's plan."

I thought that over. "I don't know that he's of any more use here than out there on his own. As long as they don't grab him. In any event, I'm not even sure what our next move is. I feel like we need to take a more direct approach."

"More direct how?"

"If we stop Joth, we end the whole problem."

"Stop him like . . ."

"I'm just tossing that out there."

"Well, you can't just toss it out there. Stop him how?"

"I guess there are a few ways. We could try to get other execs at Plexol to comprehend what he's doing and stop him. But honestly, I don't expect much from those clowns. As long as Joth is bringing in money what do they care. So then there's the more direct approach. Capture him and keep him somewhere until we've managed to remove his virus once and for all. But then as soon as we let him go he'll go right back to working on his plan."

"So then . . ."

"Well, killing him seems a little drastic. Then again, he is about to take over the entire world and turn us all into zombies under his direct control. So from a historical perspective, maybe the real question is why not kill him."

"I don't like that option."

"Ok, well feel free to pitch a few of your own."

"How about a political approach. Part of his plan is taking over the voting process. What if we managed to control it, then used the political power to . . . do something."

"Yeah. Even if we managed to take over the voting machines, we can't just sit and wait for the next election while he takes over the world. It's only a matter of time until he has enough people out there under his control that elections will be irrelevant."

"Ok, so then what's the solution?"

We both sat back and thought. For me it was not exactly thought so much as allowing my mind to drift around the problem and look at it from different angles. Technologically we were not making enough progress. Politically we were not going to get anywhere. Where was the answer. I paid attention to my breathing. In and out. I let myself relax into it, stopped trying to control everything and just drifted into existing. Time passed but I have no idea how long.

Max came out from the other room.

"That was an amazing nap."

"I was wondering what had become of you," Heather said.

"I definitely needed to recharge. Any new messages on the brain chip?"

"Not that I noticed."

"That's odd." Max sat at the console and looked over the message log. "Nothing. That's weird. I wonder how often he sends messages. Maybe somehow we lost our link. Maybe he figured out we were monitoring it and cut us off."

"Quint and I were talking."

"Yeah?"

"He thinks maybe we need to take a more direct approach to the Joth problem."

"Direct like kill him?"

"That was on the list of options, but I don't think it's a realistic choice. Or a desirable one."

"Ok, so then what's another direct approach that would be realistic and desirable."

"That's kind of where we got stuck."

"I'd say stuck is about where we are. I have an idea, but I think it probably falls under the undesirable heading."

"Unfortunately all our options do. What were you thinking?"

"We blow up the servers."

"Like, with a bomb?"

"Yeah."

"You're right, that is not desirable. I think it also fails the realistic test."

I stood up and walked over to Max, looking at the console. "We do have a direct link into Joth's servers."

Max looked up at me, then back at the screen. "What are you thinking, some sort of power overload? You know as well as I how many safeguards they have built into the system to prevent that."

"I know they do on the main Plexol servers. But who knows how Joth set up his own little pool of machines, or who set it up for him. He definitely didn't anticipate anyone knowing about let alone gaining access to his servers. If we can run enough routines simultaneously, even if we don't damage the hardware, we could at least keep the server locked up with useless tasks. He would be unable to monitor the status of the virus or send out messages. That would enable us to remove the virus."

"Or get our messages to the brain chips. If we control that army, it opens up a lot of new possibilities."

The 3 of us sat and pondered this. Max turned to the console, opened a new program, and started writing some code. I sat down at the laptop. "Max, you work on the loops, I'll throw together something that keeps our little tunnel to the server open even if the attack is detected."

Heather got up from the couch and went into Nacho's room. Max and I would compare notes from time to time, then dive back into the code. I liked working with him. He had a very similar coding philosophy to mine.

After about an hour of solid coding he was beta testing his code. Mine was still a bit of a mess. Heather came out with Nacho. "Hey guys, I have a little something to add to this plan."

"We'll take all the help we can get."

"Quint, what you said about an army got me thinking. Nacho has hundreds of little robots all over the place. What if we sent them down to Joth's servers, loaded with small explosives. Even if only a few made it, the ones that arrived would self-destruct. That could put a little damper on things."

"Heather, I've said it before and I'll say it again. I love your brain."

"But where do we get enough explosive material?" Max asked.

"You guys let Nacho and me work on that. You keep working on the code. Between the 4 of use we're bound to make some progress on slowing down Joth."

And so we all went to work. I was a little jealous that I hadn't thought of the robot idea. The more time I spent around Heather, the more I was realizing she was the smartest of the 3 of us. And definitely the easiest on the eyes.

Max finished testing and tweaking his code, so I gave him a chunk of mine to work on. Nacho left for a while, I assumed in search of something to make the robots a little more destructive. Everything seemed to be coming together, but in the back of my mind I knew it had seemed that way before, and somehow Joth had remained a step ahead of us.

Nacho came back and huddled with Heather while Max and I finished up. We ran a few tests on my code, then compiled it together with Max's code. We uploaded the whole package to Joth's servers and set it running. Max then tried to open a new session on Joth's server, but was unable to connect, which we took as a good sign. Max switched over to the laptop.

"Let's send a standard cyberverse connection request from the brain chip and see what happens."

"Good thinking."

"Looks like it's just spinning its wheels. The chip can't connect."

"Hopefully that means it can't receive any messages either."

"Of course, it's only a matter of time before Joth figures out what's going on and has one of his programmers ferret out our code."

"That's fine, it throws a nice monkey wrench into the works. Let's see if Heather and Nacho need any help."

Nacho was on the floor with a soldering iron. Heather was

sitting at a small table, attaching what looked like blobs of yellow clay to small wheeled robots. I picked up a blob and she grabbed my hand. "Careful, that stuff is volatile."

"How big a blast can we expect from each blob?"

"Any one of these is enough to take out the whole server room. I don't want to take any chances. We'll have 30 robots in total. All we need is one of them to make it to the server room and we're golden. We already know we can get close through the vents. Even if the robot can't get through the vent into the room, we would really just need 3 of them to go off to completely destroy the servers."

"What can Max and I do?"

"Work on the decision tree for finding the server room. We'll program it in so that if we lose communication with the robots they still have good odds of completing their mission."

"And what if they blow up in the wrong place?"

"All three of us were down there, we all got tours, and none of us saw anyone down there except Kett and Joth. I suppose it could cause some structural damage to the building, but that far below the main lobby it's not a huge risk. We aren't going to topple the whole place over."

Max and I worked on the decision tree, working through possible difficulties the robot could encounter in locating the server room on its own. We drew out maps of the portion of the basement we had been through and used that as the basis for the path the robot would take. When we finished we wrote it out as code and then used a broadcaster to beam the instructions to each of the robots.

The robots themselves also carried transceivers as well as cameras so we could drive them remotely as long as we maintained contact with them. That would be tricky considering how deep underground they were going.

I sat down with Heather and we worked out the launching spot for the robots. The easiest place was from the lower level parking garage and into the ventilation system. None of us had a car, but we could get a rental. Nacho volunteered to get the car and meet us downstairs with it. Then we would go to the launch sight together.

While Nacho was off getting the car, Heather, Max and I carefully packed the robots in blankets, which we then put into several bags. Next we needed to disguise our appearance as much as possible to avoid being spotted on the way to Plexol. We found hats and put them on. Max had a pair of sunglasses he put on, and I tossed a scarf around my face. Heather laughed.

"That scarf is definitely you. You look like a terrorist."

"As long as I don't look like me we're doing ok."

When Nacho got back he called up and told us there was a slight problem. We came down with the bags full of robots to see for ourselves. There was a nice big dent in the front of the car.

"You rented a damaged car?" I asked.

"No, on the way here I ran into a cement guard rail."

"Hm. Perhaps I should take over the driving."

Nacho got out and I took over. It had been a long time since I'd driven a car and he had to show me where some of the controls were. Heather and Max piled into the back and off we went. It was a bit of a herky jerky drive, but I didn't run into anything. I looked around at the people we passed. How many of them had brain chips? How many were out looking for us, trying to stop us from helping them.

We got stuck in traffic as we got closer to Plexol and I started to get paranoid about someone looking in the car and recognizing us. Nacho must have been thinking the same thing because he started flipping switches until he found the one that tinted the windows. Unfortunately he also turned on the sound system at full blast and was having a hard time figuring out how to turn it back off. After a few more tries he got it.

I entered the parking garage at ground level and took the ramp down to the lowest level we could get to. There was another ramp going down to the next level, but it was blocked by a chain link fence on wheels. There were no guards but there were cameras. I turned around to look at Heather and Max.

"We've got two options, we can put the robots into the vents at this level and hope they make it down to the next one, or we can drive through this fence, but that will alert Joth and Plexol security to our presence."

Max looked the fence over and said, "I think there might be another way. These usually have a remote option. If I can find the access code we can open it from here."

He pulled out his p-rom, key chip, and a small transmitter chip, hooked them up together, and started running a program to test codes randomly. He looked up at me. "They usually don't have a lock out for multiple attempts. But if we don't get it soon we should just bust through since sitting here has to be arousing suspicion anyway."

Suddenly the gate opened. I drove through and down the ramp. We were at the lowest floor. I recognized the elevator door down there. Heather and Nacho got out while Max and I kept a lookout. Heather pried the grate off the vent and Nacho carefully loaded each of the robots inside. Heather pushed the grate back in place and they jumped into the car. Max already had the remote out and was starting to guide the robots to their destination. Nacho looked over his shoulder but when he saw that Max was doing a good job of it, he settle back. I kept a lookout for any signs of trouble.

"We should think about getting out of here soon," I said.

"Just give me a couple more minutes. This is going to work a lot better this way than relying on the robots to find their own way, and I don't think we'll be able to control them from outside."

"Is it safe for us to be down here when the explosion goes off?"

"That I'm not so sure about."

"Well, get them close enough that they can find it themselves, then let's go."

"Agreed."

Max concentrated on getting the robots to the server room.

Heather, Nacho, and I kept lookout. It was surprising no one had come down yet to ask us what we were doing, but Plexol security probably didn't monitor this area very well. I wasn't sure if Joth had set up his own cameras down here, but if he did, he probably didn't want to come out in case we had come to get him. He could send Kett, but perhaps he was off doing something else. I had no idea if Josie was still working for him or not. She was probably off on a new mission by now, maybe miles away.

"Ok, let's get out of here," Max said.

I didn't need to be told twice. I shoved the guide stick forward and we lurched back up the ramp. The gate was closed again but this time I wasn't waiting. I accelerated and drove right through it. The gate when flying off to the side as we raced up the ramps and out of the parking garage. Max called out "I've lost control of them, but they were very close, they should be there any—"

There was a loud explosion and what felt like a small earthquake, followed by loud sirens. I quickly merged into traffic and got us out of there, heading back to Nacho's place. We passed police speeding the other way but they showed no interest in us.

Back at Nacho's apartment we turned on the holo-viewer to see coverage of the explosion. So far it seemed they weren't sure where the explosion happened in the Plexol building, which was being evacuated. Emergency crews were shown running all over the place as 100's of Plexol employees poured outside.

"We should contact the media," Heather said.

"And say what?" I asked.

"Tell them this was done by . . . the Anti Brain Chip League."

"The ABCL?"

"Got something better?"

"Let me think about it."

"The point is, the story is on now. If we link it back to the brain chip then that story gets more attention."

"Yeah, it also leads the authorities right back to us. It's one thing dealing with Joth and his army of sheep. It's quite another dealing with the entire state security apparatus. They're a little touchy about acts of terror."

"Wait, maybe we don't need to call them. Look."

It was Sam Peters. Heather turned up the sound. He was saying, "still no word from authorities whether this act of terror is linked to the allegations that Plexol's brain chip causes memory loss, but those we've spoken to say they're leaving no stone unturned."

"I guess Sam's not as dumb as he looks," I said.

"I think he's kind of cute," Heather said. I gave her a look and she grabbed my hand. "Don't worry, Quint. I think you're cute too."

"Thanks. I think."

"Anyway, this was a big success. We should celebrate."

"Not so fast," Max called from the console. "I'm getting a transmission to the brain chips. A new message."

"But how, we blew up the servers," I said.

"He must have a backup system somewhere. It's coming online. The message is just a head count, establishing contact with all operational brain chips and checking their status."

"Is there a way to trace where the message is coming from?"

Nacho walked over and flipped a switch on the back of the white cylinder. A new window opened on the laptop. He smiled. "There you go, longitude and latitude. Type in #map."

Max typed it in and another window opened with a map showing the location of the backup servers. It was about 500 miles away. We all looked at it. Nacho asked, "so . . . put together another batch of robots?"

"We don't even know what that place is," I said.

"Zoom in."

As Max zoomed in we could see the image of a warehouse out in the middle of nowhere.

"We may not need robots this time," I said. "He probably doesn't have anyone out there guarding the place. We could just take some explosives and a remote detonator out there and blow the whole place up. But we need to get there before Joth or anyone working for him does."

Nacho went to the back room and came out with a small suitcase. "Here's the rest of the explosive, it should be enough to do the job. I can program the detonators on our way there. Let's get going. Who's coming?"

We all stood up and walked to the door without answering. Soon we were back on the road. Max and Nacho were in the back working on the detonator, Heather was keeping me company in front. She had a utili-chip with the map on the monitor. She plugged it into the chip port so the display came up above the windshield. Once we got outside the city I was able to speed up and let the car steer itself. I turned to Heather.

"You know, part of me feels like we keep getting closer to finishing this job, and part of me . . ."

"I know what you mean. But we have to keep trying."

"I think I would have given up long ago if it weren't for you."

She smiled at me, then leaned over and gave me a kiss.

"Hey," I said, "I'm trying to drive here."

"Looks to me like the car is driving."

"Well, I'm trying to look like I'm driving."

"Great job."

We zipped along. The map showed us closing in on the warehouse, and before long we could see it off in the distance. At first there didn't seem to be anyone else around, but as we got closer I spotted Joth's car parked outside.

"He's already here," I said.

"Well that makes things messier," Heather said, "what do we do with him?"

"Maybe we just threaten to blow it all up, and get him to shut it down."

"And then what, take him with us? Take him somewhere else and leave him in the middle of nowhere?"

"That could work. Then go back and blow it all up."

"What if there's someone else with him?"

"Then we've got a problem."

I pulled up next to Joth's car and got out, leaving the others with the car and the explosives. I walked around to the side of the building and peaked in the door. It took my eyes a second to adjust. When they did I saw Joth talking to Kett. They turned and looked at me. Then everything went black.

10.

I woke up in the back of Joth's car. Josie was next to me. At first I was so disoriented I was actually happy to see her, but as my head cleared and I realized what was going on it was all I could do to keep from biting her. In the front seat Joth was driving and talking to Kett.

"They're still behind us, I can't lose them."

"So what. We'll deal with them when we get to the hideout."

"What if they have weapons?"

Kett turned back and saw I was awake. "How 'bout it Quint. They got any weapons?"

"He won't tell you anything," Josie said.

"Oh, sorry Josie, I didn't mean to bother your little boyfriend there."

"Don't start with me Kett. It's not too late for me to snap your neck for real."

"Would you two stop it, I'm trying to drive. Kett's right, we'll have to take them to the hideout and take our chances there. Are either of you armed?"

"I've still got some of Kett's toys from his stash, but the only useful thing in there was a the laser grenade, and I used that long ago."

"Well I've got a laser gun, but I don't think we want to be getting into a shootout when we don't know what they have. Let's get inside the hideout, shut the door before they can get in, and hang out with code boy here. If they have more explosives it won't do them any good. They can't blow us up while we have their buddy with us."

"Sounds like our best chance at this point," Joth said. "As long as we can keep them outside long enough, we can call in reinforcements to attack them."

"Calling in your zombie army, Joth?" I said.

No one bothered to answer, and we rode the rest of the way in silence. I looked back and could see Max driving with Heather beside him. Nacho was in the back, probably rigging something up. I could see the look of concern on Heather's face and wished I could contact her. Then I remembered the com-chip she had given me when I'd gone to News 10. I reached in my pocket to find it, but it was gone. They'd emptied all my pockets. I stared at Josie but she wouldn't look at me. I continued to glare.

"So, it's just about money? You're willing to do this just for a chip full of credits?"

She didn't answer.

"You know, I used to make a lot of money, but one day my

conscience got the better of me. I couldn't take the meaninglessness of chasing more credits while draining away my soul. Every day I pissed away coding for Plexol was another day of life I'd never get to live. I can tell you, no matter how difficult things got drifting around, the freedom was worth it. It took me a long time to figure out, but I finally did."

She turned to me. "Quint, spare me the lecture. I don't need some loser telling me how to live, or what's important, or what great wisdom he found at the bottom of a dumpster. I've already made my choices. If you think you can change me, well, you're even more hopeless than I thought."

I waited for the usual wave of pain that came with rejection from Josie, but there was nothing. Her words were meaningless to me. She was meaningless to me. Finally, I truly was free. How many years had I carried her around, letting her tear me apart from the inside out. But now that virus was gone. The host was healthy. I turned back and looked at Heather, and locked eyes with her. I gave her a smile, and slowly she smiled back.

I turned back to Josie. "You know, he's just using you."

"Thanks for the warning."

"I don't know what he's promised you for helping him out, but you're unlikely to get any of it. Joth is only focused on himself. He'll never share power with you."

Josie looked at Joth, then back to me. "Joth is a genius. He's going to take over this whole planet. He'll need my help to run things."

"No he won't. He's got an ever growing army of zombies out there that will do whatever he tells them to do. He has no respect for anyone other than himself. He's going to use you until he doesn't need you anymore. And then he'll stick a brain chip in you and send you on your way to become one more brainless sheep."

"So I guess your point is I should join you and your crew of geeks. And then what. What do I get out of that?"

"Nothing Josie. You'll get nothing no matter what you do, because you are nothing. You have no heart, no sense of joy. So there's nothing in this world that's ever going to make you happy. For you it's just a matter of degrees of unhappiness. Fear, hatred, and suffering. Of course, there's a way out of all that, but I doubt you'll find it on your own."

"And I suppose you have the key to that."

"Not just me. Lots of people. But not Joth. All he has is more fear, hatred, and suffering. Anyone who feels the need to control the entire world is obviously so trapped in his own attachment that he can't see the reality right in front of him. All he can give you is more delusion. Even if his plan succeeds, what has he achieved. He'll have destroyed all that matters, all that's good, all that's human, and be left controlling a world where nothing happens. Where there's no spark of creativity, no surprise, no life. What's the point of that?"

"Why should I listen to you, Quint. What have you ever achieved?"

"I guess it depends on how you measure achievement. Really, it depends on why you're bothering to measure achievement in the first place. What is it you're keeping track of, Josie. What is it you're trying to achieve. And how will you know when you get it?"

"That's all just chitter chatter. I live for action. I'm at the center of something brilliant and new, something that will transform the world."

"Into what?"

She turned away from me and looked out the window. Joth called out, "almost there." In the distance I saw another warehouse, similar to the last one. He sped up the car but Max was still close behind. As we got closer to the building he slammed on the brakes. As soon as the car stopped, Joth and Kett jumped out and opened the door to the warehouse. Josie grabbed me, pinned an arm behind my back, and shoved me to the door. Kett grabbed my other arm and helped shove me into the warehouse. Once in they slammed the door shut and bolted it. I heard Max slam to a stop outside and car doors opening. Joth yelled out, "we've got your friend Quint, so don't do anything stupid."

Kett moved to a monitor and flipped it on. We could see Heather and Max circling the building, looking for another entrance. Nacho was still in the car, but I couldn't see what he was doing. Joth walked over to a group of servers and checked to make sure they were running. Josie kept close to me but had let go of my arm. I looked around for a way to escape, but the bolted door seemed to be the only way out. There was no way for me to get to it, unbolt it, and get out before Josie would grab me.

"Shit," Joth yelled out. "There's something jamming the signal. It must be the guy in the car, he has some gear in there. Kett, go out there and shut him down."

Kett moved to the door and unbolted it. As soon as he had it open I ran for the door. Josie was right behind me. I grabbed Kett and swung him around into Josie, knocking both of them over, ran outside, jumped into our car and peeled out. I pulled around to the back of the building and stopped so Heather and Max could jump in. Then pulled back to the front.

"Max," I yelled, "get Joth's car, he left the key chip in there. Then follow me. We need to get some distance between us and them, they have a laser blaster."

Max jumped into Joth's car and got it going. Josie and Kett were running over to him, so I steered straight for them and gunned it. They ran back into the warehouse and shut the door. Max was already driving off and I followed behind him. When we were a safe distance away we pulled over. Nacho was still working in on gear in the back seat and I left him to continue that. Max, Heather and I got out to talk.

"As far as I can tell this is the last of the servers. If we blow these up the whole operation is done."

"Max and I already dropped explosives around the building. We should detonate them now."

"I'm not so sure. If we do that we kill 3 people. Maybe the threat of blowing it all up is the better option."

"That requires we communicate with them."

"Ok, hand me a com-chip and I'll see if they're in a talking mood."

I took Heather's chip and contacted Josie. She answered. "Nice move Quint, but you can't get near us without getting shot."

"Josie, you're surrounded by explosives. All three of you stay in the building. If anyone comes out, we detonate. Tell Joth to turn off the servers."

"How do I know you're telling the truth."

"Well, the only way to prove it is by blowing you to bits. If that's the path you want to take, just let me know."

"You wouldn't have the guts."

"I might not, but my friends are raring to go. Just give them an excuse, Josie, and you're all charred atoms."

I could hear her talking to Joth. After a moment Nacho popped out of the car. "They've stopped attempting to broadcast. I can't tell for sure if the servers are off, but I'll know if they try to get a message out again. From this distance I can't jam the signal, but I can detect it."

Josie got back on the com-chip. "The server is off. So now what. We all just sit here forever?"

"Sounds appealing but I have another idea. You guys come out 1 by 1 with your hands up, then lay face down where we can see you."

"Yeah, I don't think that sounds like such a good idea. You got what you wanted. The server is off. We're going to wait this out here. If you guys get bored, feel free to go home."

I turned off the chip and looked at Heather and Max. "Well, now what?"

"She's right," Max said, "we're at a bit of a stalemate. We need a way to get them out of there. Preferably not with laser's blasting our direction."

"I have an idea," Nacho said. "we can rig some smoke bombs. All we need to do is get one in there and smoke them out."

"Do we have everything we need for that?" asked Heather.

"Unfortunately no, but I can drive into town and get what we need while you guys stay here and keep them inside. I'll leave the remotes for the explosives just in case. And you can detect any transmissions with this."

Nacho noticed something on the monitor and clicked a few buttons. "Uh oh. Looks like they got a transmission out right before we told them to shut the server down. Joth is calling in the troops."

"What do you mean?" asked Max.

"That's what he means," said Heather, pointing down the road. There was a long line of vehicles heading our way. "I think it's safe to assume those people aren't coming out here for a family picnic."

"Ok, so now what do we do," asked Nacho.

I looked at the transmission receiver. "Any way we can rig this thing to send a message out?"

"Yeah, but there's no way we can transmit to the brain chips with just this," said Nacho. "We need access to the server. We need to get in there and take control. But how. We can't get them to come out. Even if we did, it would take a while to jack into the server, get set up and send a message. We just don't have time. I think we need to run, regroup, and then try again."

"We could still blow up the warehouse," said Heather.

"That doesn't solve our zombie problem," I said. "Without the server we have no way to get them to stop pursuing us."

"Then let's get out of here," she said. "He can split up, lead them on a wild goose chase, get the smoke bomb supplies and come back."

"Let's do it," I said. Max and Nacho took Joth's car, Heather and I took the other car, and we were off. Heather kept an open com link to Nacho. We headed for town and at first the traffic continued passing us in the other direction. Then Nacho said over the com, "Joth is sending out a new message, they'll be blocking the road. Looks like it's going to be a bumpy ride." Seconds later the traffic in front of us fanned out to block the entire road. I drove off the road onto the shoulder, then onto the dirt. The car bumped along, occasionally hitting a small hole or hill that would jar us. The cars spread out farther and farther so that I had to keep going off across fields to try to get around them. We were now heading perpendicular to the path we needed to take to get back to town.

Heather called over to Nacho, "this isn't working, we'll never get anywhere this way, and if they circle around us we're trapped. Let's head back to the warehouse. We'll break in and fight it out with Joth and company. If all else fails, we blow the place up. At least we'll take Joth with us, and this nightmare will be over."

"I don't like that plan," Nacho said.

"Got a better one?"

"I knew you were going to say that."

Heather turned to me. "Any thoughts?"

"Baby, I'm just trying to keep this thing from flipping over. If you want to head back to the barn, just give me the word."

"Let's do it, we're running out of options here."

I turned back toward the warehouse. There were cars ahead of us on the road so it was going to be bumpy fields all the way. Nacho turned to follow us. A string of cars had beat us there and was circling the warehouse to protect it. It looked like this option wasn't going to work either.

"Ok, now what?"

"We still have the option of blowing the place up," said Heather.

"Now we'd be killing innocent people along with Joth's crew."

"It might be our only choice. I don't know what else to do. We can't fight our way through all those cars and people. They've got us cut off."

"Oh my god, that's it," I shouted. I changed direction again and headed for the closest utility pole. Heather grabbed my arm.

"Quint, are you nuts? You'll get us killed."

"Nope, this car has about 100 air bags ready to deploy. It won't be fun, but we'll survive. More importantly, we'll take out the power to the warehouse."

"I'd like to do more than survive Quint."

"Like the lady says, you got a better idea?"

"Yes. We can blow the pole up." She got on the com-chip and called over to Nacho.

"Head over to the utility pole, and have an explosive ready, we're going to knock out their power."

"Can do."

There was a trail of cars following us but no one between us and the closest utility pole. Heather said, "we'll have to peel off and get them to follow us so Nacho has time to set up the explosives."

"Ok, here we go."

I turned off and headed once more for the warehouse, figuring the zombies were more likely to protect the warehouse than go after Nacho. I figured right. Soon the cars were either swarming around the warehouse or chasing behind us. Meanwhile, Nacho had made it to the utility pole and was out of the car. I took a loop around to the other side of the warehouse, which was now protected 6 cars deep. Then I looped back. Nacho was back in the car with Max, driving off. I headed away from the warehouse with a long trail of cars behind me. Suddenly there was a loud explosion and we saw the pole shoot up about 5 feet in the air, then crash down, taking the power wires with it. There were huge electrical sparks like lightning, then nothing. Suddenly the cars that had been following me turned off toward the warehouse.

"They must have a default command to protect the warehouse if they stop receiving updated orders," said Heather.

"Let's get out of here. There's no way he can repair that pole. Without electricity all they can do is sit inside the warehouse, surrounded by an army of confused people."

But just then some of the cars started turning toward us again. Nacho's voice came over the com-chip. "He must have switched on a battery backup, he just sent out new orders for them to follow us and destroy us."

"Quint did you see anything in there that looked like a battery," asked Heather.

"Everything was covered over with tarps. I have no idea what's in there, but Joth doesn't leave much to chance. If he has a battery backup, it can probably last at least a day. I don't think I want to spend the next 24 hours being chased all over the globe."

Nacho's voice came over the com again. "Look guys, I think we need to blow up the explosives. I see three options. Find a way to lure all those people away from the warehouse, get the explosives inside the warehouse, or just blow it up as is."

"Well, I don't like the 3rd option," said Heather. "How can we get the explosives inside when there are so many people surrounding the place?"

"As far as we know those people are just looking for you 3. I could be just another mind chip user as far as they can tell. I could walk up, gather the explosives, somehow pry the door open and toss them inside, then run like hell and detonate."

"I don't like that one either. How do we lure them away?"

"No idea. Their current order is to protect the warehouse.

What if they saw a threat to the warehouse but at a distance. They would go there to try to stop it."

"Ok, so we get some sort of weapon, or something that looks like a weapon. But what if only some of them go to where that is and the rest stay put."

"Then let's take the opposite approach," said Nacho, "We leave. The threat is gone. They abandon the warehouse and go back to searching for you guys. And then we detonate."

Heather turned to me. "What do you think Quint?"

"I can't think of anything better. I take it we're now ok with the idea of killing the 3 people inside the warehouse?"

"I don't see much choice. As long as Joth is alive he'll be a threat. He can always put together a few servers and go right back to his plan."

"And after we kill them, then what. We would all be murderers. Where do we go, how do we live?"

"Quint, I don't care about us anymore. We have to stop Joth."

"Well I do care about us. I care about you. I don't want you throwing your life away. I say we go back to the apartment and find a way to hack into the server. Shut it down that way. Nacho can stay here with the detonator just to continue the stalemate. The 3 of us go back and work at it with a tech approach. It's what we do best. We aren't killers."

"We aren't killers, but we aren't quitters either. One way or another, we have to stop Joth. Forever. Our best chance to do that is . . . look. They're leaving the warehouse. They're coming toward us."

Nacho came over the com-chip. "Joth instructed them to take the explosive devices and drive toward us. We just lost a lot of options. Now what?"

I turned to Heather. "Let's get the hell out of here."

She said into the chip, "Let's go. Back to the apartment. We need to form a new plan. Quint wants to try another hack. We can figure out what other options we have."

We sped back to the apartment over the open fields. Fortunately most of the other cars were already near the warehouse. Once we cleared them we got back on the road. They were chasing behind us. Heather said, "so how do we lose all these people?"

"We'll have to take some local roads. They'll clog themselves up on a single lane road. Only a few cars will manage to follow us. Then we lose them."

"Sounds like a logical plan. Just do me a favor."

"What's that."

"Don't crash."

"I'm adding that to my to do list."

I headed toward town. Max was right behind me, with the next car about 10 car lengths behind us. As I got closer to the apartment I started taking side streets, even alleys, to force the cars behind us into a single file. Eventually there were only a few cars directly behind us. After more twists and turns through the local roads we lost them as well. I headed for Nacho's apartment and when we got there we parked the cars and ran upstairs.

It felt good to be back in our little sanctuary, but there was no time to rest. I got on the laptop and Max got on the console. I told him, "I'll check the log and find the IP of the backup servers they're using. You work on hacking in to either shut it down or take control of the broadcasts. I'm going to see if I can find the module that controls the battery backup and make it fail."

Heather said, "while you boys do that, Nacho and I are going to brainstorm ways to attack the warehouse and take down the server without killing anyone."

They went into the next room while we worked on the computers. Occasionally Max would have me look at something on the screen. We had found the servers and pinged them, but neither one of us had gotten inside yet. I was running a dictionary attack and trying to send in messages disguised as a response from a brain chip. Nothing was working.

Heather and Nacho came out of the room. "We're going to make a supply run, see if we can put together some remote control flying robots. Little helicopters. We'll land them on the roof, set the building on fire, and force them out that way. You guys keep working on hacking in. If you make any progress let us know."

Heather came over and kissed me on the cheek. "I'll see you, Quint."

They had been gone a full half hour when it suddenly occurred to me. The warehouse had a tin roof. There was no way to set it on fire. I pulled out a com-chip and called Heather. When she answered she sounded out of breath.

"Quint, we're in range. The brain chip army still hasn't arrived. I'm going to blow it up."

"Heather, what are you doing?"

"We brought more explosives and a new detonator, and placed them around the warehouse. I knew you wouldn't like it. But now we're just a button push away from ending this. It's all set. Here goes."

"Heather, no."

"Too late Quint. 3, 2, 1 . . ."

I heard the explosion, then a long pause. I pinged the server. Nothing.

"Heather."

"Still here Quint. It's done."

"Then get out of there. Come back."

"I'm not leaving until we see the bodies."

"Just get out of there."

"I'll call you back."

She disconnected. I continued pinging the server. Nothing. And then, after a few minutes, I received a response from a new server. Could Joth have set up an automated backup? If so, now we would have to start all over finding and destroying this one. What if there were 100 more. 1,000 more. Suddenly, Heather came back on the com.

"There's no one here. We blew up the server, but no bodies. They must have left after we did."

"Heather, a new server came up. I'm going to try to locate it. You and Nacho get back here now."

"We're on our way."

Max and I went to work trying to locate the new server, but it seemed to have no fixed physical location. Max said, "maybe it's in a truck. It could be anywhere. I'm beginning to think Heather was right. We should have killed Joth when we had the chance."

"I'm still not convinced. But it's a moot point. We need a fresh approach here. Obviously there's a detection scheme in place that lets him know when a server goes down, and switches to a new server. If we can hack into that and trick it into thinking the current server is down, we can set up a fake server and get it to switch over to the fake. Then we can take over the broadcast capability."

"That sounds pretty iffy. You work on that, I'm going to try to hack into the new server. I was starting to make some progress on the last one before Heather blew it up. I can take what I learned from that one and apply it to this one."

We continued working for another half hour. At that point I took a break and tried to contact Heather. But there was no answer. Max watched me as I tried again and again to contact her. He got up and pulled out his own com-chip. He tried both Nacho and Heather. Nothing.

11.

We took Joth's car and headed toward the warehouse. Max had the laptop and the white cylinder. He was trying to get a fix on the new server's location but it kept shifting around erratically. When I arrived at the warehouse there was no one there. Just the remains of the warehouse and the burnt out server. I turned back and drove towards town. Max said, "all the signals are in town. Maybe it's not a moving server. Maybe it's several servers networked together wirelessly. The program is being run across all of them, with a central processor somewhere splitting up the processing tasks."

"Ok, so where do we find Heather and Nacho?"

"Joth likes to keep his enemies close. So the real question is, where would he be?"

"Probably with one of those servers. He had to come out here to capture Heather and Nacho. He would have gone to the nearest server to hide out there. Plot a map of all the signals your receiving, we'll check the closest one first."

Max had the map in a few minutes and gave me directions to the server's location. I sped up. Max said, "Quint, what if they aren't there?"

"Then we check the next closest place. And the next."

"No, I mean, what if . . ."

"You can't think that way."

"I can't help thinking that way."

"If Joth has harmed them, he will pay for it."

We rode the rest of the way in silence. I pulled up to the new location, a tall gray building just outside town. There was a camera above the front door. I pulled around back and looked for another way in. There was a fire escape up the back of the building. "Let's try that. We can look in the windows on each floor as we go up and see if we can find them."

I pulled over and we started up the fire escape. The building looked abandoned until we got to the 5th floor. Through the window I could see light coming from underneath a door. I raised the window and turned to Max.

"I'm going in here, but it may be a trap. You try one floor up, then work your way back down here."

He continued up the fire escape while I climbed in. I walked down a hallway to the door with the light. I listened carefully but couldn't hear anything. I lay down on the floor and tried to see under the door but the gap was too small. I got back up and quietly tried the door knob. It was locked. I walked down the hall and tried the next door. It wasn't locked. I slowly opened it and looked around, then flipped on the light.

The room was empty except for a desk and chair. I searched the drawers of the desk but it was empty. I pulled out the large bottom drawer which had a locking mechanism. There was a long thin piece of metal along one side, which I bent back and forth until it broke off. Then I used it like a drill, slowly digging a hole through the wall adjacent to the room with the light. I moved it around slowly, trying not to make too much noise. I pushed it through the drywall and pulled it out. When I looked through it was dark, so I figured there must be another layer of drywall a few inches away. I stuck the metal rod through the hole again and twisted it around until I could see light coming through the hole. I was about to start again when I heard someone at the door. I hid behind the desk and waited. The door opened and I saw someone approaching. When he came around the desk I jumped up and was about to attack when I realized it was Max. He jumped back but managed to squelch a shout. I pointed to the hole in the wall and he peeked through. He whispered, "I can't see much."

"Working on it."

I went back to drilling, slowly opening up the hole until it was big enough to look through. The lit room was empty, but there was a door to another room. I looked up and saw the usual ugly drop ceiling. I signalled to Max to help me move the desk over to the wall, then I stood on it and pushed up the tile. I climbed up and onto the dividing wall, crawling over and lifting a panel so I could see into the lit room. Empty. I dropped down to the floor, then unlocked the door. Max came around and walked in, then I checked the next door. Locked. Max gave me a boost back up onto the wall and I crawled over to the next room, slowly lifting another ceiling tile and peeking in. Kett, Heather, and Nacho were in there. Kett was sitting on a chair facing them. They were both sitting on the floor. I lowered the tile and crawled along the wall until I was close to where Kett was sitting, then dropped down to the floor. Kett stood up and spun around, and I nailed him across the jaw with a punch that hopefully hurt him as much as it hurt me. It felt like I'd broken on of my fingers, but I drew back and took another slug at him. This one hurt me twice as much, but he looked dazed. Nacho was on his feet and grabbed Kett from behind, pinning his arms. I took a shot at his gut and when he slumped down I searched him for weapons. There was a laser gun, which I took. Heather ran over and hugged me, then signalled to be quiet and pointed at the next door. I tried it, but it was locked. Then I remembered Max. I opened the door to the lit room and let him in. Heather whispered, "Josie and Joth are in the next room with one of the servers. I heard them talking. It's part of a virtual server farm. Taking this one down will do us no good. We need to know where all of them are."

"Then our best bet is to take the system over and get control of his brain chip army. I'll drop into the room and get them against the wall, then open the door and let you guys in. Max can plug in to the server directly and worm his way in. Nacho, you keep lookout to make sure no one is coming to find us here. Heather, you work with Max on hacking in."

Nacho gave me a boost up and I crawled over to the next room, once more carefully lifting a tile and peeking in. I could see Joth, but not Josie. I was about to drop down when I was kicked in the back. I turned around to see Josie. She sprang at me, landing on top of me and dropping us both down to the floor, which knocked the wind out of me. I grabbed the laser gun from my coat and jammed it into her rib. She got up and backed away. I tried to get a gasp of air into my lungs. I waved the gun at Joth and signalled for him to stand next to Josie against the wall. When I could breathe again I stood up and opened the door. Max and Heather came in and immediately got to work on the server. I grabbed a chair and sat down, keeping the laser gun levelled at Josie. She was a far bigger concern than Joth. I could see the gears spinning in her head, looking for a way to attack. Joth slumped down and sat on the floor.

"You can slow me down at best, but you can't stop me. You're wasting your time."

"I disagree, Joth. I think we can stop you right now. All I have to do is kill you."

"You won't do that."

"Try me."

I saw Josie twitch, but she stayed put. Her body was tense. I knew at any moment, as soon as I dropped the gun lower, or looked away, she would make her move. I stood up, keeping the gun pointed at Josie.

"Josie have a seat, you're making me nervous."

"I prefer standing."

"I didn't ask what you prefer. Sit down."

She started to crouch, then leapt at me, grabbing at the gun, trying to twist it out of my hand. I tightened my grip and then felt a blast go off. Josie gasped and staggered back. Her left hand was gone, just a charred spot at her wrist indicated where it used to be. She stared at it, wild eyed. Then looked at me. The room filled with the stench of burnt flesh. She held up her arm. "Look what you did. Look what you did you idiot. You . . . you . . ."

She leapt at me again and this time grabbed my throat with her remaining hand, squeezing with all her strength, knocking me to the floor. I kicked at her but she was possessed. Her grip tightened. She jammed her knee into my gut and knocked the wind out of me. I pressed the laser gun to her head but she didn't flinch.

"You won't do it, Quint. You haven't got the balls."

I tried to pull her hand away with my free hand, but it felt like steel. I moved the gun to her wrist and blasted, severing her hand, which slowly loosened. I kicked her off of me and struggled to my feet, gasping for air. Heather ran over and helped me up. Max grabbed Josie and pulled her away, but she swung around and kicked him away. The pain she was experiencing from the two laser blasts either hadn't registered or she was able somehow to fight through it. Both hands were gone, but that didn't seem to slow her down. Max got up and charged Josie, knocking her to the ground and pinning her. She fought and fought but he kept her down.

"Josie," I yelled. "Stop fighting already. You're beat."

"You'll have to kill me if you want me to stop fighting."

"That's stupid. Joth can't possibly be paying you enough for this."

"It's not about money, Quint. It's about winning. It's about never quitting."

"So how exactly are you winning right now?"

She smiled a wicked smile that gave me chills. I looked around the room. The door was open and Joth was gone. I raced out into the hallway where I found Joth fighting Nacho. I jumped on Joth's back and knocked him to the ground. Nacho looked dazed.

"You got here just in time. I'm not much of a fighter."

"Grab his arm and help me drag him back into the server room."

Together we pushed and dragged Joth back to the room. Max was still holding Josie down. She seemed to have calmed down, but I couldn't be sure if she was worn out or just saving her strength for another attack. Joth sat down next to Josie.

"Great job Josie. You were supposed to keep them busy while I escaped."

"You should have had plenty of time. Don't blame me for your failure."

"You've failed me throughout this project. If you had killed

Quint back when you had the chance I'd be getting on with my plan instead of dealing with this mess. But no, you wanted me to try to bring him into the fold, add him to the team. Why on earth did I listen to you."

"I guess you're weak."

"You bitch. I don't even know who's side you're on anymore."

"My own. And right now the best thing for my side is to bring this party to a close."

She rolled over knocking Max to the ground, and I saw a laser grenade between her arms. She tossed it in the air, then got up and ran for the door. Joth ran after her. Heather jumped and caught the grenade, then threw it out the door after them. A split second passed and then an explosion knocked me over. There was bright light and a deafening sound. I shielded my face as I fell. I felt debris flying by in a big whoosh, and then it was calm again. I opened my eyes and looked around. Heather was lying face down on the ground. I ran to her and gently roller her over. She opened her eyes and looked up at me, then smiled. She said something but I couldn't hear her over the loud ringing in my ears. She slowly got up and looked around. Max stood up from behind the server and waved. Heather looked relieved. Then we looked over at Nacho who was crouched on the ground. He looked up and saw us all, sheepishly smiled, and stood up. The 4 of us looked out the doorway into the next room. There was blood everywhere. I walked out into the next room. There were a few random bits of bone and burnt flesh. The stench was unbearable. I ran through the room out into the hallway. No sign of anyone. I came back and said, "I think they're both dead," but I couldn't hear the sound of my own voice. I dragged a finger across my throat to indicate that Josie and Joth were dead.

Heather came over to me and hugged me. Tears were pouring out of her eyes. I held her tight. We stayed that way for a long time, and it felt good holding her. There was so much I wanted to say, but I knew she couldn't hear me, so I thought it all and hoped she was thinking and feeling the same things I was. Max picked up the laptop, typed a message on it, and held it up to show me. It said, "I had just gotten into the main server when you started fighting with Josie. Would you like the honors?" He switched to a window that showed the program that was coordinating the server farm. I typed in the command, "quit." The server next to us shut down. I handed the laptop back to Max and he attempted to ping the servers. None responded. It was finally over. I shook Max's hand, shook Nacho's hand, grabbed Heather and kissed her on the lips. In that moment everything felt right.

12.

Back at Nacho's we checked the white cylinder to confirm the brain chips weren't receiving any more commands. In the days that followed, we managed to interest the media in the brain chip story. We showed them the servers and documentation of the digital dementia caused by the Plexol brain chip. Plexol went on the defensive, but it was too late. With the media on our side, their market value plummeted, and with it their power. Eventually the company went bankrupt.

The old voting machines were replaced with new ones that were supposedly hack proof. That sounds like an invitation to hack them if you ask me, but hopefully it will be a while before anyone figures out how.

After all the dust settled, I moved in with Heather and she, Max, Nacho, and I started a small tech company. Who knows. Maybe someday it will be as big as Plexol. I sure hope not.

Dr. Weinberg trained a team of doctors to perform brain chip extractions and by the end of the year they were all removed.

Hopefully people will think twice before trusting their brains to a huge faceless corporation. But then, people are people, always looking for the next big thing. The next big thing for Dr. Weinberg will be finding a way to reverse the brain damage. He says he's making progress.

There's lots of ways to make money, lots of ways to live your life. In the end you're not going to keep either one. Your atoms just go back into the stew and where they end up from there I don't really know. Maybe in the end none of it matters. But for now it all matters. Now is all that matters. I feel like I went from nothing to something. From 0 to 1. I can't explain how it happened, I just know it did.

Max V. Weiss

Made in the USA
Lexington, KY
15 January 2016